当代文学名著英译丛书

汉英对照

贾平凹散文选

贾平凹 著

胡宗锋 [英]罗宾·吉尔班克 译

陕西师范大学出版总社

图书代号：WX18N1746

图书在版编目（CIP）数据

贾平凹散文选：汉英对照/贾平凹著；胡宗锋，（英）罗宾·吉尔班克译. —西安：陕西师范大学出版总社有限公司，2019.1（2020.1重印）
ISBN 978-7-5695-0338-8

Ⅰ.①贾… Ⅱ.①贾… ②胡… ③罗… Ⅲ.①散文集—中国—当代—汉、英 Ⅳ.①I267

中国版本图书馆CIP数据核字（2018）第239896号

贾平凹散文选　汉英对照
JIAPINGWA SANWEN XUAN

贾平凹　著
胡宗锋　[英]罗宾·吉尔班克　译

选题策划	刘东风　郭永新
责任编辑	张　佩
责任校对	陈君明
封面设计	白砚川
出版发行	陕西师范大学出版总社
	（西安市长安南路199号　邮编710062）
网　　址	http://www.snupg.com
印　　刷	陕西龙山海天艺术印务有限公司
开　　本	889mm×1194mm　1/32
印　　张	9.875
插　　页	2
字　　数	210千
版　　次	2019年1月第1版
印　　次	2020年1月第3次印刷
书　　号	ISBN 978-7-5695-0338-8
定　　价	58.00元

读者购书、书店添货或发现印刷装订问题，请与本公司营销部联系、调换。
电话：（029）85307864　85303629　传真：（029）85303879

目录

Contents

城

- *002* 西安这座城
- *014* 我的小学
- *034* 西大三年
- *042* 说棣花
- *080* 我的故乡是商洛

物

- *092* 丑石
- *100* 一棵小桃树
- *112* 残佛
- *122* 溪流
- *128* 文竹
- *138* 陶俑
- *156* 壁画
- *166* 不能让狗说人话
- *174* 动物安详
- *184* 荒野地

003   The City of Xi'an

015   My Primary School

035   Three Years at Northwest University

043   Happenings in Dihua

081   Shangluo is My Homeland

093   An Ugly Stone

101   A Little Peach Tree

113   Deformed Buddha

123   Streams

129   Asparagus Fern

139   Pottery Figures

157   Wall Paintings

167   You Cannot Let Dogs Talk like People

175   Animals at Ease

185   The Wild Land

情

- 194 两代人
- 200 我不是个好儿子
- 218 写给母亲
- 226 在女儿婚礼上的讲话

思

- 234 说话
- 242 辞宴书
- 250 朋友
- 262 敲门
- 272 秃顶
- 282 吃烟
- 286 龙年说龙

- 300 孤独地走向未来

195   Two Generations

201   I am not a Good Son

219   Written for My Mother

227   Speech on my Daughter's Wedding

235   On Talking

243   On refusing an invitation to a banquet

251   On Friends

263   Knocking at the Door

273   Bald Head

283   On Smoking

287   Talking about the Dragon in
         the Year of the Dragon

301   Walking into the Future Alone

城

The City

西安这座城

我住在西安城里已经二十年了,我不敢说这座城就是我的,或我给了这座城什么,但二十年前我还在陕南的乡下,确实是做过一个梦的,梦见了一棵不高大却很老的树,树上有一个洞。

在现实的生活里,老家有满山的林子,但我没有觅寻到这样的树;而在初做城里人的那年,于街头却发现了,真的,和梦境中的树丝毫不差。这棵树现在还长着,年年我总是看它一次,死去的枝柯变得僵硬,新生的梢条软和如柳。

我就常常盯着还趴在树干上的裂着背已去了实质的蝉壳,发许久的迷瞪,不知道这蝉是蜕了几多回壳,生命在如此转换,真的是无生无灭,可那飞来的蝉又始于何时,又该终于何地呢?于是在近晚的夕阳中驻脚南城楼下,听岁月腐

The City of Xi'an

I have been living in the city of Xi'an for twenty years; I dare not say that this city belongs to me or what I contribute to it; but two decades ago, when I was still in the countryside of southern Shaanxi, I dreamt about a tree which was not so tall but very old. There was a hole in the tree.

In real life, there are forests all over the mountains in my hometown, though I have not been able to find such a tree. When I first lived in the city as one of its residents, I discovered this very tree on the street. That is true. It was absolutely identical to the one in my dream. This tree continues to grow. Every year I always inspect it once every year. Its dead branches stiffen, yet the new growth remains as supple as a willow.

I often stare at the empty cicada shell which has been cast off on the cracked surface of the trunk, and spend a long time feeling puzzled. I wonder how many times one cicada can shed its casing. A life which entails such a metamorphosis is really fascinating because there can be no birth without death. But where are the flying cicadas born and where do

蚀得并不完整的砖块缝里，一群蟋蟀在唱着一部繁乐，恍惚间就觉得哪一块砖是我吧，或者，我是蟋蟀的一只，夜夜在望着万里的长空，迎接着每一次新来的明月而欢歌了。

我庆幸这座城在中国的西部，在苍茫的关中平原上，其实只能在中国西部的关中平原上才会有这样的城，我忍不住就唱起关于这个地方的一段民谣：

八百里秦川黄土飞扬，

三千万人民吼叫秦腔，

调一碗黏面喜气洋洋，

没有辣子嘟嘟囔囔。

这样的民谣，描绘的或许缺乏现代气息，但落后并不等于愚昧，它所透发的一种气势，没有矫情和虚浮，是冷的幽默，是对旧的生存状态的自审。我唱着它的时候，唱不出声

they die? At dusk beneath the setting sun to the south of the city wall, I listen to a group of crickets sing intricate melodies in the time-worn crevices within the brickwork. In a trance, I feel that this brick is me or that I am one of the crickets, staring up at the expansive sky each night, crooning as I greet every bright moon.

I am glad that Xi'an lies in the west of China, on the vast Guanzhong Plain. In fact, only on such a plain in the west of China could a city like this exist. I cannot help but break into a folk ballad about this place:

Loess drifts over the Qin land of eight hundred li,
Thirty million Qin folk roar out local opera,
A bowl of sticky noodles fills them with glee,
But having no pepper makes them complain.

Such a folk ballad may lack modern ambience, but backwardness in itself is not tantamount to ignorance. The power it radiates, however, is neither hypocritical nor superficial. Through scrutinising how people used to live it generates a cold humour. What I cannot communicate by merely singing the ballad is the moving and tragic story behind it——Kua Fu chased after the sun and ended up dying from thirst on the way to the sea. With this thought in mind, a few years ago I felt I had to refuse an invitation extended to me by several people from the South of China. They head-hunted me and dangled before my face offers of sumptuous and superlative hospitality. I turned them down and would not go because I love Shaanxi; I love the city of Xi'an.

的却常常是想到了夸父逐日渴死在去海的路上的悲壮。正是这样，数年前南方的几个城市来人，以优越异常的生活待遇招募我去，我谢绝了。我不去，我爱陕西，我爱西安这座城。

我生不在此，死却必定在此，当百年之后躯体焚烧于火葬场，我的灵魂随同黑烟爬出了高高的烟囱，我也会变成一朵云游荡在这座城的上空的。

当世界上的新型城市愈来愈变成了一堆水泥，我该怎样来叙说西安这座城呢？是的，没必要夸耀曾经是十三个王朝国都的历史，也不自得八水环绕的地理风水，承认中国的政治、经济、文化的中心已不在这里了。但可爱的是，时至今日，气派不倒的、风范犹存的、在全世界的范围内最具古城魅力的，也只有西安了。它的城墙赫然完整，独身站定在护城河的吊板桥上，仰观那城楼、角楼、女墙垛口，再怯弱的人也要豪情长啸了。

大街小巷方正对称，排列有序的四合院和四合院砖雕

The City of Xi'an

I was not born in Xi'an but I shall die here. After my eventual passing, my corpse will be incinerated in the crematorium; my soul will climb out of the high chimney riding on the black smoke; I shall become a cloud wandering over the city.

As new cities in this world increasingly resemble a heap of cement, how can I describe the city of Xi'an? There is no need to boast about how Xi'an was the capital of thirteen historical dynasties or how the eight waterways which wove around Chang'an endowed it with an enviable *feng-shui*. As time has gone by, it is true that Xi'an no longer forms the political, economic and cultural centre of China. And yet the most sublime thing is that to date, the city still allures with its ancient charm and elegance. Across the entire world, Xi'an alone retains the most rarefied atmosphere of any classical metropolis. The city wall is outstandingly intact. When one stands alone on the drawbridge above the moat and raise your head to survey the gate-tower, turrets and crenellations, even the most timid of people cannot help but burst into loud, passionate rhapsodies.

The streets and lanes are geometrical and symmetrical; the neatly and decently appointed square residential courtyards conspire with the iron-complexioned gate piers beneath the carved eaves of their entrances to transport one into an ancient world. That world is populated with stately and strong horses pulling large wooden carts. Given the opportunity, one could begin to note thousands of streets names from within the city: Examination Hall Gate (Gongyuanmen), Scholars'

门楼下已经黝黑如铁的花石门墩,可以让你立即坠入古昔里高头大马驾驶木制的大车开过来的境界里去。如果有机会收集一下全城的数千个街巷名称:贡院门、书院门、竹笆市、琉璃街、教场门、端履门、炭市街、麦苋街、车家巷、北油巷……

你突然感到历史并不遥远,以至眼前飞过一只并不卫生的苍蝇,也忍不住怀疑这苍蝇的身上有着汉时的模样或是唐时的标记。现代的艺术在大型的豪华的剧院、影院、歌舞厅日夜上演着,但爬满青苔的如古钱一样的城墙根下,总是有人在观赏着中国最古老的属于这个地方的秦腔或者皮影、木偶。他们不是正规的演艺人,他们是工余后的娱乐。有人演,就有人看,演和看都宣泄的是一种自豪,生命里涌动的是一种历史的追忆,所以你也便明白了街头饭馆里的餐具,碗是那么粗的瓷,大得称之为海碗。

逢年过节,你见过哪里的城市的街巷表演着社戏,踩起了高跷,扛着杏黄色的幡旗放火铳,敲纯粹的鼓乐?最是那土得掉渣的土话里,如果依音写出来,竟然是文言文中极典雅的词语:抱孩子不说"抱",说"携";口中没味不

Academy Gate (Shuyuanmen), Bamboo-ware Market (Zhubashi), Glazed-ware Street (Liulijie), Military Training Ground Gate (Jiaochangmen), Imperial Attire Inspection Gate (Duanlimen), Charcoal Street (Tanshijie), Wheat Straw Street (Maixianjie), Carters' Inn Lane (Chejiaxiang), Northern Oil Lane (Beiyouxiang) ...

One suddenly feels that history is not so distant. Even when an insanitary fly zooms before your face it is tempting to suspect that it too bears the imprint of the Han or Tang Dynasties. Modern entertainments are customarily staged in large deluxe theatres, cinemas, and song and dance halls. At the foot of the city wall, where mosses form a carpet like timeworn coins, there will always be spectators watching the most ancient local Qin opera, shadow displays, and puppet shows. These folks are not professional actors or artists; they simply dabble for pleasure in their spare time. Someone puts on a performance; someone else is sure to appreciate it. Performers and audience alike find an outlet for unburdening their pent-up pride. A seam of historical memory surges through the daily lives of Xi'an people. You may, therefore, be able to understand why among those utensils used by food vendors on the street the porcelain bowl that is so hefty and thick-sided is referred to as *haiwan* ("bowl as vast as the sea").

When festivals come around, have you ever seen any other city where people will perform folk opera and walk the streets on stilts? They carry apricot yellow flags and banners and blunderbusses, and thump out drum music without any other instrumental accompaniment. The

说"没味",说"寡";即使骂人滚开也不说"滚",说"避"。

你随便走进一条巷的一户人家中,是艺术家或者是工人、小职员、个体的商贩,他们的客厅必是悬挂了装裱考究的字画,桌柜上必是摆设了几件古陶旧瓷。对于书法绘画的理解,对于文物古董的珍存,成为他们生活的基本要求。男人们崇尚的是黑与白的色调,女人们则喜欢穿大红大绿的衣裳,质朴大方,悲喜分明。他们少以言辞,多以行动;喜欢沉默,善于思考;崇拜的是智慧,鄙夷的是油滑;有整体雄浑,无琐碎甜腻。

西安的科技人才云集,产生了众多的全球著名的数学、物理学家,但民间却大量涌现着《易经》的研究家,观天象,识地理,搞预测,做遥控。你不敢轻视了静坐于酒馆一角独饮的老翁或巷头鸡皮鹤首的老妪,他们说不定就是身怀绝技的奇才异人。

清晨的菜市场上,你会见到人手托着豆腐,三个两个地

most intriguing thing is the local dialect. If written out phonetically, this is revealed to consist of very elegant words from classical Chinese: folks do not speak of "carrying" (*bao*) a child, but "conveying" (*xie*) it; where their mouths cannot detect flavour they do not say "tasteless" (*mei wei*), but "numbed senseless" (*gua*); even when they spew curses they do not say "bugger off" (*gun*), but "skedaddle" (*bi*).

When people casually drop in at a house on a lane, whether the householder is an artist, an ordinary worker, a junior clerk, or a self-employed peddler, the living room must have elaborately decorated scrolls and paintings hanging from the walls; likewise tables must be festooned with choice specimens of ancient ceramics. In their daily lives it is expected of them that they should at least have a basic understanding of calligraphy and painting and of how to preserve cultural relics. Men admire black and white, while women prefer striking red and dazzling green. The people here are straightforward and honest, uninhibited about how they express joy and woe. They are taciturn, yet demonstrative, savour silence, are agile of thought, worship wisdom, and deplore wiliness; they have a heroic vigour untainted by trivia and affectionate display.

Xi'an now abounds with high-tech personnel. Many world famous mathematicians and physicists were born here. However, among the populace there are still plenty who are familiar with the *Book of Changes*. They can observe celestial phenomena and discern the *feng-shui* of the landscape, foretelling the future and exercising telepathy. One

立在那里谈论着国内的新闻。关心国事,放眼全球,对于他们似乎是一种多余,但他们就有这种古都赋予的秉性。"杞人忧天"从来不是他们讥笑的名词,甚至有人庄严地提议,在城中造一尊巨大的杞人雕塑,与那巍然竖立的丝绸之路的开创人张骞的塑像相映生辉,成为一种城标。

整个西安城,充溢着中国历史的古意,表现的是一种东方的神秘,囫囵囵是一个旧的文物,又鲜活活是一个新的象征。

should never underestimate an older man who drinks silently alone in the corner of an inn or an aged woman with white hair and a wrinkled face. Maybe they are masters who possess peerless gifts.

In the early morning at the vegetable market, you will spot people clutching blocks of tofu in their hands, chitchatting about domestic news. The residents of Xi'an have no genuine need to bother about state and international affairs. Nonetheless, they have an innate instinct which causes them to care. This has been passed onto them by the ancient capital. They do not mock the proverbial "man of Qi who feared the heavens would tumble down." Some people have even solemnly proposed that a huge statue of him be erected in the citycentre alongside that of Zhang Qian, the pioneer of Silk Road. These would become symbols of the city.

The aura of ancient Chinese history permeates Xi'an City. Taken collectively, it appears to be an ancient relic, but it simultaneously forms a lively and fresh symbol.

我的小学

小学是在寺庙里，房子都老高老高，屋脊上雕着飞龙走兽，绿苔长年把瓦槽生满，有一种毛拉子草，一到雨天，就肉肉地长出半尺多高来。老师们是住在殿堂里，那里原先有个关帝爷，脸色枣一样红，后来搬掉了，胎泥垫建了院子，那一对眼珠子，原来是两个上了釉的瓷球，就放大门口的照壁顶上，夜里还在幽幽地放光。两边的廊房，就是教室。上课的是高年级学生。台阶很高，我可以双脚从上边跳下来，但却跃不上去。每次要绕到山墙角儿，却轻轻松松地从那一边石头铺成的漫道上单脚蹦上去。那山墙角地是一棵裂了身子的老苦楝树。树顶上有个老鸦巢，筛筐般大，巢下横枝上吊着一口钟，钟敲起来，那一家老鸦却并不动静，这奇怪使我不解了好几年呢。

五岁那年，娘牵着我去报名，学校里不收，我就抱住报

My Primary School

My primary school was set up inside a temple; the building was very tall, with carved flying dragons and running beasts along the beams. The crevices between the tiles were grouted with green moss all the year round. On rainy days, a fleshy kind of weed called groundsel shot out from the earth and seemed to grow half a foot in height. The teachers lodged in the temple lofts. In former times there had been a statue of Guanyu there, the face of which was as red as a date. Later on, people moved it away and constructed a courtyard on the muddy foundations. Originally, the eyes of the deity were made of glazed porcelain beads, but then they stood it on the top of the screening wall at the entrance, where its corneas still emanated a faint light in the dusk.

The rooms on either side of the courtyard served as classrooms. Only students in the senior grades took lessons. The steps were extremely steep. I could jump down them with both feet, but couldn't scale them in the same way. Every time, I had to make a detour around the corner of the wall. From there I could easily hop along the stone-paved path on one foot. At the corner of the wall was an ancient chinaberry tree with a

Folk Temple

cracked trunk. A crow's nest as large as a sieve balanced up in its canopy and underneath that there hung a bell, which whenever it was struck never appeared to ruffle the family of birds. For a few years, I wracked my brain over this queer phenomenon. At the age of five, my mother hauled me over to enrol. The school refused me at first and so I clasped onto the leg of the office table and wailed. The teachers all around me laughed and then relented. I was not officially registered as pupil. Instead, they admitted me as a "probationer" in the reception class. My mother insisted that I should kowtow to the teachers and so I kneeled and my head made a thudding sound as it struck the floor. A female teacher scooped me up and I was worried that she might be about to tug at my ears. Her plump and meaty hand pinched away some nasal snivel. "You are a student now. How can you still have a runny nose?" Everybody guffawed and I lost face. From then on, being afraid that mucus might drip down again, but having no handkerchief, I carried a pocketful of poplar leaves. I spruced myself up every time I entered the building.

As there were few classrooms and we were the reception grade, there were no seats for us in the temple courtyard. We had to be taught in the Liu Family Memorial Hall outside the religious house. A blackboard was suspened there and some earthen bricks were stacked up so as to support a table top. When the river bed dried up in summer, the villagers tore the planks away from the bridge to serve as our desks. Each of us had to bring along our own stool. At that time my extended

名室的桌子腿哭，老师都围着我笑；最后就收下了，但不是正式学生，是一年级"见习生"。娘当时要我给老师磕头，我跪下就磕了，头还在地上有了响声。那个女老师倒把我抱起来，我以为她要揪我的耳朵了，那胖胖的，有着肉窝儿的手，一捏，却将我的鼻涕捏去了。"学生了，还流鼻涕！"大家都笑了，我觉得很丢人，从此就再不敢把鼻涕流下来。因为没有手巾，口袋里常装着杨树叶子，每次进校前就揩得干干净净了。

因为学校教室少，因为我们是一年级学生，那寺庙的大院里没有我们的座位，只好就在院外的一家姓刘的祠堂里上课。祠堂里抹着一块黑板，用土坯垒起一些柱墩儿，村子里就将夏天河面上的木板桥拆了，架在上边做了课桌。凳子是自带的。我们那时没分家，堂兄堂姐多，凳子有限，我常常抢不到凳子，加上我个子矮，坐在小凳子上又趴不到桌面上，就一直站着听课。实在腿困了，就将家里的劈柴拿来一根，在前后的柱墩上掏出窝儿架好，骑在上边。这种凳子虽然不舒服，但坐上去却从来不打瞌睡。只是课余时间，同学们都拿着凳子在祠堂后的一个土坡上反放着，由上往下开汽车，我只好圪蹴上往下滑，常常把握不好，就一个跟头滚下

My Primary School

family had not been divided into nuclear households, and having so many older paternal cousins but not enough seats to go around, I often went without. What is more, owing to my height, when I sat on a low stool it was hard for me to reach up to the desk and I was forced to stand up during lessons. If my legs became numb I would scavenge a chopped wooden stake from home and drive both ends into the stacks. The batten duly served as my seat. Uncomfortable as it was, I never dozed off in that position. My only regret was that after class I couldn't join in the others' games. They liked to turn their stools upside down and slide along the slope behind the hall playing "cars". I could only squat and ride my backside. Many a time I lost balance and somersaulted down, receiving a face full of dust.

As there was no clock in my home, we could not keep abreast of time in the morning and so more than once I was late getting up. After crying and nagging my mother, she would rise in the early hours and set about stitching shoe soles under the light of a lamp, while waiting for the peal of the school bell. In winter, when we got out of bed, the moonlight was still strong and we would yell out for our classmates in the village and accompany each other to school. Everyone had a satchel apart from me. My mother gave me a square of cloth to bundle my things tightly together and tuck under my arm. At that time I was very eager to outdo others, though fell short in this respect. Mother told me that this couldn't be helped because we had no money to spare. When we arrived the door of the hall was locked and the monitor, who wasn't

去，弄得一脸的泥土。

　　家里没有表，早晨总估摸不了时间，有几次起床迟了，就和娘哭闹。娘后来一到半夜就不敢睡，一边在灯下纳鞋底儿，一边逮那学校的钟声。到了冬天，起来得早，月亮白花花的，我们就在村里喊着同学一块儿去。大家都有书包，我没有，娘将一个小包袱皮给我，严严实实包了，让我夹在胳膊下，我那时很要强，唯这一点总不如人，但娘说没有钱，我也没了办法。祠堂的门关着，班长带着钥匙，他还没有来，我们就在祠堂前跳起舞来。跳的是新学的"找朋友"："找呀找呀找朋友，找到一个好朋友！"大家很快活，有时找着小霓，有时找着芳芳，就一对一对跳起来。到了三年级以后，这舞就不跳了，而且男的和女的就分开来。我曾经和芳芳一块踢过毽子，同学们都说我和芳芳好，是夫妻，拿指头羞我，我便和芳芳成了仇人。等到班长来了，开了祠堂门，我们就进去坐在自己的座位上。祠堂里还黑隆隆的，因为没灯，少半时候，我们点些松油节取亮，大半时候就摸黑坐着。黑板上边的墙头上，那时还留着祠堂里的壁画，记得是《王祥卧冰》，虽然不懂得具体意思，但觉得害怕。大家坐下后，都不敢靠墙，也不敢提说那壁画，就闭着眼睛把课

there yet, had the key. We would begin to dance a jig we had just learnt called "Looking for Friends": "Look for, look for, look for a good friend! At last we've found one!" Everyone was merry. Sometimes I took Xiaoni as my pal and sometimes Fangfang. Then we would pair off and dance.

By the time we reached the Third Grade, we had stopped this kind of horseplay and boys and girls would sit apart. Once, I played dropkick the shuttlecock with Fangfang and my classmates teased me and referred to us as "husband" and "wife". They shamed me by dabbing an accusing finger against their cheek and that began my estrangement from her. When the monitor came and opened the door we would file in and assume our seats. As there was no source of light it was still pitch dark inside. On occasions, we would burn pine tar, but most of the time we fumbled our way to sit down in the blackness. There were friezes painted on the walls of the memorial hall and I can remember the legend of the dutiful Wang Xiang lying down to melt the frozen lake so he could catch a fish to feed his father. Not being able to understand the underlying meaning, this filled us with fear. While sitting there, nobody dare lean against the walls, nor mention the contents of the frescoes. We just closed our eyes and began to recite our text from lesson one. As soon as one student fell silent, the rest followed suit and a hush descended on the hall. The wind rattled away at the hemp paper covering the window lattice, making everyone come over petrified again. All at once, the recitations resumed, our voices becoming ever louder so as to fortify us. Otherwise, if one was to flee the rest would follow and I would be the

文从第一课一直背诵下去。一旦一个人停下来，大家就都停下来，祠堂里静悄悄的。风把方格子窗上的麻纸吹得哗哗响，大家便又都害怕了，一哇声再背诵开来，声越来越高，全为了壮胆。要不，一个忽地跑出去，大家就都往外跑，我常常跑在最后，大呼小叫，声都变了腔。祠堂前的平台下就是荷花塘，冬天里荷花败了，塘里结了冰，大家就去那芦草窝里掏一种鸟儿，或许折下那枯莲茎秆儿，点着当烟吸，呛得鼻涕、眼泪都流下来。

在这个祠堂内，我们坐了两年，老师一直是一个女的，就是捏我鼻涕的那个。她长得很白，讲课的声音十分好听，每每念着课文，就像唱歌儿。我从来没有听到过她这么好听的声音，开头的半年时间里，几乎没有听懂她讲的什么，每一堂却被她的声音陶醉着。所以，每当她让我站起来回答问题时，我一句话也答不出，她就说："你真是个见习生！"

见习生的事原先同学们都不知道，她一说，大家都小瞧起我了，以后干什么事，他们就朝我伸小拇指头，还要在上边呸呸几口，再说一句："哼，你能干什么，你真是个见习生！"我们就打过几次架。娘后来狠狠揍了我一次，罚我一

My Primary School

last straggler left at the end, screaming and caterwauling in unesrthly tone. Facing the platform in the memorial hall was a lily pond. In the winter when the leaves withered and the water froze, we would forage for bird's eggs there in among the reeds. Or we might snap off the dried stalks of the lilies and set them alight to smoke. Often this brought up the mucus out off our noses and made us choke with tears.

We sat in this memorial hall for two years. Our teacher was the lady who had wiped my nose. She was preternaturally white in her complexion and spoke sweetly in class. Every time she read a text out loud it was just like intoning a song. I have never heard such an alluring voice. For the first half of my school years, I barely ever understood what she was saying. Still, in every lesson I found myself intoxicated by her strains. Whenever she asked me to rise and answer a question I was totally lost for words. Then she would say: "You are a probationer through and through."

Until then, none of my classmates knew my true status, so after she divulged that everyone looked down upon me. In all the exercises we did later on they would mock me by extending just their little finger and dipping it in their saliva while humming: "Hmm, what can you do as just a probationer!" I fought with them more than once, but my mother clouted me and denied me dinner as a punishment. When my teacher heard about this, she dropped by at our home and apologized to my mother and I. She said that it was all her fault and asked if I had trouble understanding her class. I answered: "I only take in the sound of your

顿不准吃饭。老师知道了，寻到我家，向我和娘做了检讨，说是她的不对，问我是不是听不懂课。我说："我光听了你的声，你的声好听！"她脸红红的，就笑了。从此，我就下了决心，一定不落人后，老师对我格外好起来，她的声音还是那么好听，但一下课，就来辅导我，惹得同学们都眼红起来。

一年级学完后，老师对我说："你年纪小，不让你升级。"我当下就吓哭了。老师却将我抱起来，说她是哄我，宣布我再也不是见习生了。我一高兴，就叫她"姨姨"，叫完就后悔了。她却并没有恼我，还拧了我一下嘴，她笑了，我也笑了。下午，她拿着成绩单到我家，向娘夸说我乖，学习进步快，娘给她打荷包鸡蛋吃。我便大胆起来，说："老师，你的声音好听，你能给我唱个歌吗？"她就唱起来，腮帮上深深显出两个酒窝，唱完就格格地笑。

到了夏天，学校里中午要睡午觉，我们就都不安分，总是等大伙伏在桌上睡着以后，就几个人偷偷到荷花塘里去玩水。胆大的都到深水里去，趴浮，立浮，还有仰浮，

voice. It is so sweet!" Red-faced, she smiled. From then on I resolved never to let myself fall behind others. My teacher too treated me more attentively. Her voice was still mellifluous, only after class she would tutor me, something which filled everyone else with envy.

After the First Grade, my teacher told me: "You are still too young. We cannot let you advance to the class above." I was scared and burst into tears. My teacher gathered me in her arms and confessed that she was just jesting and then declared I was not a probationer any more. So great was my relief that I called her "auntie." As soon as I'd blurted that out, I was struck with embarrassment. She didn't seem annoyed and simply pinched me on the mouth. She smiled and so did I. In the afternoon she came to my house with the score sheet. She praised me in front of my mother and remarked on how I had behaved well and made rapid progress in my studies. My mother poached an egg for her. Emboldened, I declared: "Your voice is so sweet. Can you sing a song for me?" As she began to trill away, two deep dimples appeared on her cheeks and she giggled afterwards.

When summertime came, we were permitted a lunchtime siesta. All of us were mischievous. While others rested their arms and heads on the desk, a few of us would slip out to the lily pond to play. The braver ones would wade in at the deep end. then doggy paddle, tread water or do the backstroke with their tiny bellies poking above the surface. Timid as I was, I would grip the roots of the tree at the margin and whip up waves with my feet. The girls would always snitched on us, causing the teacher

将小肚子露在水面。我因为胆小，总是在塘边抓住树根，双脚在水面打着浪花。那些女生就常常告发我们，老师就每次用手在我们胳膊上抓一下，看有没有水锈的白道，结果，总要挨一顿。但是，水里的诱惑力十分大，我们免不了还是要去，而且每次去时对女生晃晃拳头，再是去了将衣服藏在树丛里，跑到荷花塘深处去玩。有一次，竟被校长发现了，狠狠地批评了老师，老师委屈得哭了。我们知道后，心里很难受，去向老师承认错误。却恨起校长来，就在祠堂门前挖一个坑儿，用泥捏一个胖胖的校长，埋在里边。又是女生告发了，老师在课堂上让我们几个站起来，大发脾气，末了，查出是我的主意，就把我推出教室，将一颗扣子也拉扯掉了。下课后她给我缝扣子，我哭得泪人儿一样，连夜写了检讨书，一直在教室里贴了三天。

我那时最爱语文，尤其爱造句，每一个造句都要写得很长，作业本就用得费。后来，就常常跑黄坡下的坟地，捡那死人后挂的白纸条儿，回来订成细长的本子；一到清明，就可以一天之内订成十多个本子呢。但是，句子造得长，好多字不会写，就用白字或别字替着，同学们都说我是错别字

to scrape our forearms with her fingers to check for the telltale blanching that comes with immersion in water. Inevitably, we would end up being scolded. The water was too seductive and we couldn't tear ourselves away from it. Every time we went, we would wave our fists at the girls. On arriving, we hid our clothes among the bushes and headed for the deep end. Once, the headmaster discovered us there and he upbraided our poor teacher to the point of tears. After hearing what had happened, we confessed our crime to the teacher, though it was the principal whom we started to revile. We dug a pit before the entrance to the memorial hall and used it to bury a chubby clay effigy of him. Again the girls told on us. Our teacher asked a number of us to stand up in class and meted out a tongue lashing. Later, when she knew I was the ringleader, she pushed me out of the classroom so fiercely that I lost one of the buttons from my coat. When class was over, she did sew it back on, but my face was by now soaked in tears. Overnight, I wrote an essay of self-criticism then left it on display in the classroom for three whole days.

At that time I loved Chinese Language lessons most of all, and especially enjoyed composing sentences. Each of them I wrote was excessively long, so I got through numerous exercise books. Later, I frequented the graveyard at Yellow Slope and pilfered the white paper mourners left behind. On returning home, these would be bound into long, narrow notebooks. When Tomb-sweeping Festival came around I could bind ten volumes of this kind in a single day. Nonetheless, when I was composing my mammoth sentences there were too many

大王，教师却表扬我，说我脑子灵活，每一次作业都批"优秀"，但却将错别字一一画出，让我连做三遍。学写大字也是我最喜欢的课，但我没有毛笔，就曾偷偷剪过伯父的羊皮褥子上的毛做笔，老师就送给我一枝。我很感谢，越发爱起写大字，别人写一张，我总是写两张三张。老师就将我的大字贴在教室的墙上，后来又在寺庙的高年级教室展览过。她还领着我去让高年级学生参观。高年级的讲台桌很高，我一走近，就没了影儿，她把我抱起来，站在那椅子上。那支毛笔，后来一直用秃，我还舍不得丢掉，藏在家里的宋瓷花瓶里，到了"文化大革命"中，破起"四旧"，花瓶被没收走了，笔也就丢失了。

从一年级到二年级，我的父亲一直在外地工作，娘要给父亲去信，总是拿着几颗鸡蛋来求老师代写，老师硬是不收鸡蛋，信写得老长。到了二年级下半学期，她说："你现在能造句了，你怎么不学着给你父亲写信呢？"我说我不会格式，她说："你家里有什么事情，你就写什么，不要考虑格式！"我真的就写起来，因为家里的事我都知道，都想说给父亲听，比如奶奶的病好转了，夜里不咳嗽了。娘的身体很好，只是唠叨天凉了，父亲的棉衣穿上没有。还有家里的

characters I was unable to visualise, so I had to spell them phonetically or use homonyms. My classmates all called me the "monarch of misspelling", though the teacher always praised me for having a nimble brain. Every time my homework would be graded "excellent", but she would underline the incorrect words in red and ask me to copy them out in their proper form three times. Learning calligraphy was also a great favourite, despite the fact that I didn't own a brush. Once, I tried to snip some wool from my uncle's lambskin mattress and fashion a brush. When my teacher offered me a brush of my own, my heart was filled with gratitude and I became even fonder of that discipline. Where others would turn out one practice piece, I would produce two or three. The teacher would pin these up on the classroom wall and eventually went onto display them in the senior students' classroom inside the temple. She even led me over there for a visit. As the teacher's desk was so high, it totally eclipsed me. She picked me up and planted my feet on a chair. I continued to use that brush until it was bald and even then could not bring myself to throw it away. I hid it inside a Song Dynasty vase at home. During the Cultural Revolution, when the "Four Olds" were being smashed, that piece of china was confiscated with the writing implement inside.

From my time in the First Grade to the Second Grade, my father worked away from home. Whenever my mother wanted to write a letter to him, she would always take a few eggs to the teacher and beg her to be her scribe. She consented, but refused the gift. In the latter half of

兔又下了崽，现在一共是六只了，狗还很凶，咬伤了三娃的腿，其实是三娃用棍打它，它才咬的。还有我学习很好，考试算术得了一百分，语文得了九十八分，是一个字又写错了，信花了三天才写好，老师又替我改了好多错字，说："以后到高年级做作文，或者长大写文章，你就按这路子写，不要被什么格式套住你，想写什么就写什么，熟悉什么就写什么，写清、写具体就好了。"我从那时起就记住了老师的话，之所以如今我还能写些小说、散文，老师当时的话对我影响很大。

这一年，我们上完了二年级。三年级学生可以到寺庙大院里去住了，我们都很高兴。寒假里，同学们都去挖药、砍柴卖钱，商量春节给老师买些年画拜年。到了腊月三十日中午，我们就集合起来，拿着一卷子年画，还有一串鞭炮去找老师，但是，老师却不在。问校长，原来她调走了。校长拿出一包水果糖来，说是我们的老师临走时，很想各家去看看我们，但时间来不及了，就买了这糖，让开学后发给我们每人一颗。我们就都哭了。从那以后，我再也没有见到我的那位老师，在寺庙里读了四年书，后来又到离家十五里外的中学读了三年，就彻底毕业了，但我

the Second Grade, my teacher said to me: "Now that you can compose sentences yourself why don't you try writing to your father?" I told her that I didn't know the format. She said: "Only your family is meant to see it, so there's no need to be a stickler for the rules." I really made the effort to learn to write. Since I knew all the goings on in my family, I wanted to relate them to him. For instance, my grandma was recovering from her illness and no longer hacked away at night.

My mother was in the pink of health, though she kept on nagging that the weather was getting cold and she was worried in case my father wasn't wearing his cotton-padded clothing. Apart from that, our pet rabbit had given birth to a total of six babies. Our dog continued to be very ferocious and it had bitten Sanwa's leg. The truth was that it was acting in retaliation because he had struck him with a stick first. For another thing, I had fared well in the school examinations, scoring 100% in Arithmetic and 98% in Chinese Language. I was penalised for writing one character wrong. It took me three days to complete the letter and my teacher corrected so many spelling mistakes and said: "In the future when you advance to the higher grades or when you are grown up and want to write a long article just write in this fashion. Don't be bound by any of the formats. Write whatever you want to write and about whatever you are familiar with. As long as you can make them concerte and clear." From then on, I have borne my teacher's words in my mind. Nowadays, I am able to turn my hand to both fiction and prose all because of how her words influenced me at that time.

的启蒙老师一直没有下落。现在是二十五年过去了,老师还在世没有,我仍不知道,每每想起来,心里就充满了一种深深的惆怅。

That year we completed the Second Grade. We were elated because the Third Grade students were permitted to board inside the temple. During the winter vacation we all went to forage for herbs and chop wood for pocket money. We discussed buying some New Year pictures for our teacher at Spring Festival. On the morning of the New Year's Eve according to the Lunar Calendar we assembled with the paintings and some firecrackers with the intention of visiting her. She was nowhere to be found. We asked the headmaster and he told us she had been transferred to another place. He took out a parcel of sweets and informed us that when our teacher was leaving she really wanted to visit the home of every one of her students. Time was limited, though and so she left behind this gift to be distributed among us when the new term began. We all broke down in tears. From then on, I never caught sight of my teacher again. I studied in the temple for a further four years and then in a secondary school fifteen li away for three years. Then my schooling was complete. I never got to know the whereabouts of my first teacher. To date, twenty-five years have passed and I have no idea whether she is still in this world or not. Whenever I recall this story I come over low-spirited.

西大三年

——十五年后的记忆

一九七二年四月二十八日,汽车将一个十九岁的孩子拉进西大校内,这孩子和他的那只绿皮破箱就被搁置在了陌生的地方。

这是一个十分孱弱的生命,梦幻般的机遇并没有使他发狂,巨大的忧郁和孤独让他只能小心翼翼地睁眼看世界。他数过,从宿舍到教室是五百二十四步,从教室到图书馆是三百零三步。因为他老是低着头,他发现学校的蚂蚁很多。当眼前有了好些各类鞋脚时,他就踽踽地走了,他走的样子很滑稽,一只极大的书包皮,沉重使他的一个肩膀低下去,一个肩膀高上来。

Three Years at Northwest University

— Memories after fifteen years

On 28th April 1972, a vehicle carried a nineteen year old boy into Northwest University. The boy together with his shabby green case found himself in an unfamiliar place.

Thus far his fate had been precarious. He did not lose his head over receiving this dream-like opportunity. Acute loneliness and melancholy caused him to view the world with apprehension. He had counted how from the classroom to the dormitory there were 524 steps and how from the classroom to the library 303 steps. As he always kept his head perpetually bowed he discovered that there were so many ants scuttling across the campus. All sorts of shoes cut across his line of vision and he would stroll away reluctantly. His manner of walking was ungainly. The burden of a gargantuan schoolbag pressed one of his shoulders down, tilting the other one skyward.

He only ever mounted the stage once to participate in the choral competition. In actual fact, his mouth may have opened but no sound

他唯有一次上台参加过集体歌咏，其实嘴张着并没有发声。所以，谁也未注意过他，这正合他的心境。他是一个没有上过高中的乡下人，知识的自卑使他敬畏一切人，悄无声息地坐在阅览室的一角，用一个指头敲老师的家门，默默地听同窗的高谈阔论。但是，旁人的议论和嘲笑并没有使他惶恐和消沉，一次政治考试分数过低，他将试卷贴于床头，早晚让耻辱盯着自己。

他当过宿舍的舍长，当然尽职尽责，遗憾的是他没有蚊帐，夏夜的蚊子轮番向他进攻。实在烦躁到极致，他反倒冷静了，想：小小的蚊子能吃完我吗？这蚊子或许是叮过什么更有知识的人的。那么，这蚊子也是知识化了的蚊子，它传染给我的也一定是知识吧。冬天里，他的被子太薄，长长的夜里他的膝盖以下总是凉的，他一直蜷着睡，这虽然影响了他以后继续长高，但这样却练就了他善于聚集内力的功夫。

他无意于将来要当作家，只是什么书都看，看了就做笔记，什么话也不讲。当黄昏一人独行于校内树林子里，面对了所有杨树上那长疤的地方，认定那是人之眼，天地神灵之大眼，便充裕而坚定，长久高望树上的云朵，总要发现那云活活

was released. Nobody noticed him and inconspicuousness was exactly what he craved. He was a boy from the countryside who had never attended senior high school. This lacuna left him in thrall of everybody else's knowledge. Quietly he would consign himself to the corner of a reading room and when he had to knock on a teacher's front door he would merely poke the wood with a single pattering finger. His classmates' rowdy discussions would be audited in silence. their mockery and jeers failed to upset or dishearten him. Once he scored a desultory mark in Politics. He pasted the exam paper above the head of his bed so that the object of his shame could look down on him from dawn to dusk.

Another time he served as prefect of the dormitory. Of course, he discharged his duties with great care. His only regret was that he did not own a mosquito net. The pests assailed him relentlessly every summer night. Despite being pushed to an extreme of aggravation, he was able to regain his composure. He wondered: "Is there any way that all these tiny mosquitoes can gnaw me into oblivion? Perhaps they bit someone more knowledgeable than me first, so maybe these are wise mosquitoes? They could be passing a touch of that onto me!" In winter, his quilt was too thin. During the long night, he always felt chilly below the knee and so curled into a foetal position. This surely inhibited his growth, but must have trained him to be good at consolidating the inner power of his *kung-fu*.

He had no intention of being a writer in the future. He read any

的是一群腾龙跃虎。

他的身体先还较好,虽然打篮球别人因个子小不给传球而从此兴趣殆尽,虽然他跳不过鞍马,虽然打乒乓球尽败于女生,但是,当一次献血活动,被抽去300CC之后又将血费购买书了。不久就患了一场大病,再未恢复过来。这好,他却住了单间,有了不上操、不十点熄灯的方便了,但创作活动也于此开始。当今有人批评他的文章多少有病态意味,其实根因也正在此。

最不幸的是肚子常饥,一下课就去站长长的买饭队,叮叮当当敲自己的碗筷,而一块玉米面发糕和一勺大混菜,总是不品滋味地胡乱扒下。他有他的改善生活日,一首诗或一篇文章写出,四角五分钱的价格,他可以去边家村食堂买一碗米饭和一碗鸡蛋汤。因为饭菜的诱惑,所以他那时写作极勤。但他的诗只能在班壁报上发表。

他忘不了的是授过他知识的每一位老师,年长的,年轻的。他热爱每一个同学,男性的,女性的。他梦里还常梦到

book he could lay his hands on and jotted down notes after poring over them. All the while he remained tight-lipped about what he was doing. Ambling alone in the forest groves of the campus at sunset, he scrutinised all the scars on the bark of the poplars. It was his belief that these were sentient eyes, the eyes of the gods who governed the heavens and the earth. Feeling enriched and determined he gazed long and intently at the clouds above the trees, always perceiving in them pouncing tigers and leaping dragons.

His health was at first rather hale. As no one was willing to pass the ball to someone so diminutive, his interest in basketball soon dried up. He couldn't clear the vaulting horse and even lost ping-pong matches to female classmates. When it was time to donate blood he gave 300 cc and used all of the fee on purchasing books. Soon afterwards, he was stricken by a serious disease from which he was never to recover. That proved a blessing in disguise. He could now live in a single room, was exempted from morning exercises and not required to observe the 10pm curfew. His creative writing thus entered its gestation. Nowadays, some critics accuse his articles of having "the air of a sick man." The root cause of this is how his career as an author began.

The most unfortunate thing is that his stomach always churned. After class, he was forced to queue in a long line to buy food, clanging his chopsticks against his bowl. He would always polish off a block of cornbread very swiftly together with a ladleful of mixed fried vegetables. Anyhow, he had his own way of giving himself a treat. When a poem

图书馆二楼阅览室的那把木椅,那树林子中的一块怪模怪样石头,那宿舍窗外的一棵粗桩和细枝组合的杨树,以及那树叶上一只裂背的仅是空壳了的蝉。

整整十五年后,他才敢说,他曾经撕过阅览室一张报纸上的一块文章,而且是预谋了一个上午。他掏三倍价为图书馆赔偿的那本书,说丢了那是谎言,其实现在还保藏在他的书柜里。他是在学校偷偷吸烟。他是远远看见一个留辫子的女学生而曾做过一首自己也吃惊的情诗。

一九七五年的九月,他毕业了,离开校门,他依旧提着那只绿皮破箱,又走向了另一个陌生的地方。

or an article of his was published, he would use the 45 cents royalty to buy a bowl of rice and a bowl of egg soup in a restaurant in Bian Family Village. Owing to the seductive quality of rice and vegetables, at that time he wrote prodigiously. His poems, however, got no further than the bulletin board displayed in his classroom.

What he could never forget were all the teachers young and old. Moreover, he felt an attachment to everyone in his class, whether male or female. In his dreams, he always imagined the wooden chair in the reading room on the second floor of the library, a grotesque carbuncle of a stone lurking in the forest, the thick trunk and the wiry branches of the poplar tree outside his dormitory window, and the shattered carapace of a cicada on the leaves of the tree.

Fully fifteen years have gone by. In all that time he could not bring himself to confess that he once tore an article from a newspaper in the reading room. For the whole morning, he had plotted how he would execute this theft. He also lied about losing a library book, paying fines on it three times when it was actually still on his shelf. As a student, he had started to smoke on the sly. When he spied a girl with long pigtails tantalise his eye-line in the distance he would pen a love poem for her that would surprise even himself.

In Spetember 1975, he graduated. He left the university, still carrying his shabby green case. He was once again to find himself in another unfamiliar place.

说棣花

棣花有十六个自然村。

白家垭的白亮傍晚坐在厦子屋门槛上吃饭,正低头在碗里捞豆儿,啪的一下,院子里有了一条鱼,鱼在地上蹦。白亮以为谁从河里钓了鱼给他扔进来,就说:谁呀?!没有回应,开了院门出来看,一个人背身走到巷口了,夕阳照着,看不清那是谁,但那人似乎脚不着地,好像在水上漂,又好像是被什么抬着,转过巷头那棵柳树就不见了。

白亮想着是不是三海,他给三海家垒过院墙,三海一直感激他,钓了鱼就送了他一条?但三海害病睡倒一个月了,哪里能去钓鱼?是白路的二儿子水皮?水皮整天去钓鱼哩,钓了鱼就拿到公路上卖给过往的司机,咋能平白无故地给他一条呢?!

Happenings in Dihua

Dihua consists of sixteen hamlets.

Bai Liang from Bai Family Strip was eating supper as he sat beneath the eaves on the threshold of the side-room. While he had his head bowed down, searching for the beans in his bowl there was a slapping sound and a fish appeared on the floor of the courtyard. The fish was tossing around on the ground. Bai Liang thought that maybe someone had caught it in the river and thrown it over for him. He asked: "Who is it?" No answer was forthcoming, so he opened the door and went out. All he could see was a man with his back turned to him at the entrance of the lane. In the light of the setting sun he could not make out who that person was. The man's feet seemed not to be planted on the ground as if he was floating on the surface of some water. Or else some kind of force appeared to be carrying him. After turning around the willow tree at the entrance to the lane, he simply vanished.

Bai Liang wondered if this was San Hai. He had helped San Hai erect the walls of his courtyard and was flushed with gratitude for this favour. Was it he who had caught the fish for him? But San Hai had

白亮回到院子里再看鱼,鱼身上没有鳞片,有一小片云,如一撮棉花,知道了鱼是从天上掉下来的。

天上有银河,银河里还真有水,水里有鱼?或者,是鹤从棣花河叼了鱼飞过院子,不小心松了口,把鱼掉了下来?

白亮觉得是好事,还往天上看了许久,会不会也能掉下个馅饼,但天上没有馅饼,起了悠悠风,风把一片杨树叶子吹了来,贴在他脸上,盖了一只眼。他把鱼捡回屋里炖了。

第二天,白亮到河里担水。河边的浅水里一只猫和一条鱼搏斗,鱼可能是游到了浅水滩上,猫就去叼,鱼摆着尾打水花,猫几次都跌坐在水里。白亮放下桶去撑猫,却发现那鱼身上长了毛和翅膀,正疑惑,鱼游进深水里不见了。

鱼怎么长毛和翅膀呢?

白亮更看见了奇怪的事,几乎就在那条鱼游进深水后,突然在河上流的百米远,一群鱼从水里跃出来,竟然就飞到

been laid up ill for more than a month. How could he go angling? Could it have been Bai Lu's second son Shuipi? Shuipi spent the whole day everyday fishing. Once he caught a fish, he would take it to the highway and sell it to a passing motorist. How come he had sent him one for no apparent reason?

Bai Liang returned to the courtyard and inspected the fish. It had no scales upon its body, only a tiny cloud rested on the skin. He then realised that it had fallen down from the heavens.

People think of the Milky Way as being a silver river. Could there be fish in its waters? Or, might a crane have picked up a fish from the stream in Dihua and carelessly let it slip from its bill while flying over his courtyard?

Bai Liang felt that this was a good omen. He gazed at the sky for a long time. Was it possible that some cake could drop down as well? No cakes came, just a gust of breeze. The wind blew over a poplar leaf which covered over his face and one eye. He picked up the fish and took it inside to braise.

The next day he went with his carrying pole to collect water from the river. A fish and a cat were tussling away in the shallows by the bank, a fish and a cat were tussling away. Maybe the fish had swum to the edge and the cat had lunged down to bite it? The tail of the fish beat ripples and several times the moggy pitched backwards and got its posterior wet. Bai Liang put down his buckets and went to drive away the cat away. Remarkably, he discovered that the fish had fur and wings. As he was

Village Entrance

pondering this, the fish launched away into the depths and disappeared.

What is more, Bai Liang came across another strange thing. The moment the fish darted away, about one hundred metres upriver a shoal of fish suddenly leapt out of the water and flew into the air. Simultaneously, a flock of birds dived down from the sky and entered the river one by one. This cycle repeated itself. Birds plunged downwards and fish shot upwards. One moment they were fish; the next they were birds.

From then on, Bai Liang's behaviour and manner became different to that of other people. For example, when he quarrelled with his neighbour about the boundary line between their properties, the other fellow would curse him by saying he was a grass-reared ruminant. He would reply by saying that it was true. When the villagers heard about this, they all asked how it was that he could allow himself to be maligned in this way. He replied that he had actually been raised on a diet of grass. Were vegetables not a kind of grass? Were rice and wheat flour not made from the seed of grass? His gait also altered from before. His arms now swung back and forth wildly as if he was doggy paddling in the river. People laughed at him, but he retorted: "Do you think that air is not water?"

Wu Fu from Jiayuan Village had been practicing *qigong* for three years and gained a reputation for it. He invited some women to stand with their eyes closed and then would transmit his telekinetic power from five paces away. He asked them: "Can you feel the lick

空中，而同时空中又有一群鸟飞下来一只一只入了水。然后，轮番从天上到河里，从河里到天上，一会儿是鱼，一会儿是鸟，循环往复。

从此以后，白亮行为做事和人不一样。比如，和邻居为庄基红过脸，邻居骂他是吃草长大的，他说，是呀，吃草长大的。村里人事后说，你咋能让他那样骂你？他说就是吃草长大的呀，菜不是草吗，米和面还不是草籽磨的？他走路也不像以前的走势了，胳膊前后甩得很厉害，像是狗刨式的，在河里游泳。别人笑他，他说：你以为空气不是水？

贾塬村的五福练气功，练了三年，就练成名了。他让一些妇女闭眼站着，然后在五步之外发功，问：有凉飕飕的风吗？妇女说：啊，啊，是凉飕飕的。棣花人都知道了五福有气功，让五福用气功治病。五福治病不治头痛脑热，他觉得那不是病，喝碗姜汤捂捂汗就好了，他只治癌症。棣花患癌症的人多，没钱去省城医院动手术，而五福发功治病不收费的，说：给我传个名就行。

of the cold wind?" The women replied: "Yeah, yeah, it's come over parky." When people in Dihua knew that Wu Fu had indeed mastered *qigong* they begged him to cure their diseases. Wu Fu refused to treat headaches and fever. Those could be remedied with a bowl of ginger soup and by sweating it out under heavy quilts. Instead, he devoted his energies to attacking cancer. In Dihua many residents were afflicted with this condition. Poor as they were, most could not afford to go to the provincial hospital and receive surgery. He charged no fee for his services, merely pronouncing: "Spreading the news of what I'm able to do is reward enough."

Wu Fu was very particular about finding the correct location in which to treat patients. Usually, he would operate at the foot of the cliff behind the village. A cypress tree of more than a century old grew down there and he liked to clamber up it and gather the *qi* it gave off. He would then ask the patient to sit down as he stretched out his arms with the palms of his hands facing towards them. This served to channel the qi in their direction. On 14th July 1998, while he was doing this, a gust of wind struck up, intensifying into gale force. He was whipped off his feet and propelled violently against the cliff-face. When it died down, he broke loose and plopped down to the earth like a meat patty.

The Erlang Temple is to be found on Eastern Street and in front of it is the Scholar Deity's Tower. The two buildings are separated by a sprawling square. Local folks used to call it "the temple playground". Shuan Lao made his home behind here. He was ugly and penniless,

五福治病很讲究地点，一般都在村后的崖底，崖底有一棵百年老柏，他趴在树上要采一会儿气，再叫病人坐了，开始推开手掌，要把一股子气发出去。一九九八年七月十四，他正发功，天上起了风，风是狂风，一下子把他吹起，啪地甩到了半崖壁上。风过去了，他从崖壁上掉下来，人已经成了肉泥饼子。

　　东街有个二郎庙，庙前就是魁星楼，庙和楼中间的场子很大，棣花人习惯叫那是庙场子。拴劳住在庙场子后边，人丑，家又贫，但他有一个好被单子。整个夏天，拴劳都不在家里睡，嫌家里热，又有蚊子，天黑就披着被单子去庙场子了。他在庙场子扫一块净地，盖着被单睡下了，第二天一早，却总是从魁星楼上下来。魁星楼很高，攀着楼墙的砖窝可以上到第三层，上面风畅快。村里人都说拴劳半夜里披着被单就飞上楼了，传得神乎其神，但问拴劳，拴劳只是笑，没承认，也没否认过。

　　后来，拴劳去西安讨好生活了，走时就带着被单子，一走三年再没回来。不知怎么，村里都在议论，说拴劳在西安以偷窃为生，能飞檐走壁，因为他有被单子。

but owned a decent sheet. All through the summer he refrained from sleeping indoors because he loathed the stultifying heat and the marauding mosquitoes. Dusk would always find him heading for the playground with his blanket. After clearing a patch of ground he would bed down with it draped over his body. Nevertheless, the next morning he would be spotted climbing down from the nearby tower. The Scholar Deity's Tower was extremely tall and one could reach as far as the third storey by using gaps in the external brickwork as footholds. The wind merrily caressed the top of the steeple. Villagers surmised that Shuan Lao must fly up there around midnight and this miracle was on everybody's lips. When people asked him about the matter, he simply smiled. He would neither admit nor deny the rumour.

Later on, Shuan Lao went to Xi'an to make a living, taking his sheet with him. He was gone for three years without ever returning. Somehow the villagers still continued to gossip about him. They said that he was making a living by thieving. That sheet gave him the power to leap onto roofs and vault over walls.

In 2002, when SARS was rife, the sixteen hamlets of Dihua organised a crisis team to guard vigilantly and be prepared to fight to the last. People from Xi'an were prohibited from entering the village. It was right around this time that Shuan Lao came back. The team chased after him as one battalion and he was driven as far as the cliff on the western side of Dihua. Below the precipice ran the river. Someone declared that they should stop pursuing him, otherwise he would be pushed down

到了二〇〇二年,到处闹"非典",棣花十二个自然村组织了防护队,严防死守,不准从西安来的人进村。拴劳偏偏就回来了,防护队一声喊地撵他,撵到棣花西头的崖上,崖下就是河。有人说:不敢再撵了,再撵就掉到河里了。又有人却说:没事,他能披被单子飞天哩。防护队举着棍棒还往前撵,拴劳就从崖上跳下去了。

拴劳跳下去是死了,还是活着,反正从此再没回来过,也没有他的消息。

冬季里,崖上出现了许多蝙蝠,有人说是不是拴劳变成了蝙蝠,因为蝙蝠的翅膀张开来像是披着一块小被单子。立即有人反对这种联想:怎么可能呢?蝙蝠的被单是黑的,拴劳的被单是白的。

巩家村的上槽在给自行车充气的时候受了启发,就整天练着用手抓空气,抓一把,就扔出去砸旁边的狗,但狗总是没反应。这一天他又在练习,听到巷口有人叫他,上槽上槽,叫得生紧。抬头看时巷口起了烟,灰腾腾的,先是一股

into the water. Someone else chimed in that it didn't matter. His sheet gave him the power to float into the sky. The mob assailed him with sticks and clubs and then Shuan Lao jumped down.

Whether the fall left him dead or alive, he did not return and no news was ever heard about him.

In the winter, a profusion of bats appeared on the cliff-face. One villager suggested that they were the reincarnation of Shuan Lao. When the bats spread their wings it appeared as though they were carrying a tiny sheet. At once, another voice objected. The bats' sheets were black, whereas his was white.

Shang Cao from Gong Family Village had a flash of inspiration while pumping up his bike tyre. From then on, he practiced a particular *kung-fu* move everyday – grasping a handful of air and then flinging it like an invisible projectile at the dog. The dog, however, made no reaction. One day when he was practicing, he heard someone calling for him from the entrance to the lane: "Shang Cao! Shang Cao!" The tone was urgent. He raised his head to find that a plume of grey smoke was rising up then billowing in his direction. When this reached his feet, it dawned on him that it was a dog. Another wisp of smoke had already reached the top of his head. He grasped for a broom and struck out at it. Unexpectedly, a pigeon dropped down. The bird flapped its wings on the ground for a while before flying away. Two twists of smoke duly appeared and inched towards him. He thought: "What could they be?" On peering at them with fixed eyes, it transpired that it was his pa

冲过来，到跟前了，却是一只狗。再是一疙瘩烟已经到头顶上了，拿了笤帚便打，竟然打着了，掉下来一只扑鸽，扑鸽在地上扑腾了一阵，又飞走了。后来有两团烟相互交融纠结地过来，他想着：这是啥？定睛盯着，两团烟是他大他妈，背着两篓子红薯，惊得他张嘴叫不出声了。

他大说：十声八声喊不应你？到地里背红薯去！

上槽瓷着眼看他大他妈，还用手扇了一下，他大他妈不是烟呀，烟一扇就散的。

他大说：你咋啦？

上槽说：哦，我眼睛雾很。

他大说：年轻轻的雾啥眼？

上槽要放下笤帚，笤帚突然软起来，一溜烟从指头缝里飘了去。而且看巷口外的路上，烟雾更浓，烟里有乱七八

and ma approaching him. Both of them had a basket of sweet potatoes on their back. His mouth was agape, yet he was too startled to utter a sound.

His ma said: "I called you eight or ten times, but not a peep. I wanted you to go to the field and fetch sweet potatoes."

Shang Cao stared at his parents and swished his hand before his face. His pa and ma were not smoke that could be batted away.

His pa asked: "What's the matter?"

"My eyes have become foggy."

"You are so young. How could this happen?"

He laid down the broom. It suddenly became soft and slipped through his fingers like a plume of smoke. On looking at the road by the entrance to the lane, the smoke and fog became more intense. A sound of people bustling about could be heard from within the pall. One may as well be blind for all the good having eyesight does for you in the darkness of evening. When he sat by the door he could tell who was coming by the noise their footsteps made on the village path. Now he could work out that the folks who were talking were his second great uncle, Laixi's father, his wife, Chun Cao, and Auntie Chan. Even though their voices were audible, the people themselves were invisible. Every last one of them had become just a column of smoke, whether thick or thin. They took the shape of either a cotton cloud or strip.

Shang Cao followed all the columns of smoke. For a while they assumed the shape of a human being, then reverted back to smoke.

槽的人的声。平日在夜里，夜即便黑得像瞎子一样黑，他坐在院门口，村道里一有脚步声，他也就知道这是谁来了。现在他听出说话的有二爷，有来喜伯和他老婆，有春草、蝉婶子。但他能听见声音就是看不到人，人都是一片子烟，或浓或淡，是絮状也是条状。

上槽就跟着那片烟走，一会儿看见他们有人形了，一会儿又都是烟。

上槽最后是从巷口走到巷外的土路上，一直到了河滩地，背了那里挖出来的一篓红薯。往回走时，却不知道怎么回去，因为他发现村子的那个方向并没有了村子，新有的房子，树，连同土路，除了烟，都不见了。立了好久，那烟像蘑菇一样隆起，在空中酝酿翻腾，忽然扑蹋下去，渐渐地又变成房子，树，还有直直的一条土路，土路上蹦着蚂蚱。

上槽把他看到的情景告诉给村人，村人全是一个口气，说你眼睛有毛病了。上槽就觉得自己眼睛肯定有毛病了，不出半年，眼睛便瞎了。

Happenings in Dihua

Shang Cao walked from the entrance of the lane to the road outside. He continued until he reached the field by the riverbank, carrying from there a basket of sweet potatoes on his back. As he was making his way home, he abruptly lost his bearings. There was no village in the direction from which he had come. The newly-built houses, the trees, and the earthen path had all disappeared, leaving nothing behind except for smoke. He stood there for a long time. The smoke rose up like a mushroom, seething and somersaulting. All in an instant, it came crashing to the ground. Gradually, another metamorphosis occurred; the smoke being transformed back into houses, trees, and straight earthen paths. Grasshoppers were bounding about the path.

Shang Cao told the villagers what he had experienced. All the folks agreed that there must have been something wrong with his eyes. Shang Cao then felt certain that there was a problem with his vision. Within half a year he had become totally blind.

Elm Liu, the son of the Liu Family from Middle Street Village, had a name that was not propitious. Elms trees always grow in a disobedient way. For over thirty years, Elm Liu refused to obey his Pa. When the sun came out and he asked him to hang out the quilt, he would instead build a chicken coop. When his Pa told him to sow peppers, he would plant potatoes.

On reaching the age of 56, his Pa became afflicted with ascites in his belly, and was seized by the desire to build his tomb on Cow Head Slope behind the village. After all that was where all the villagers were

中街村刘家的儿子名字没起好，叫刘榆，榆树总是拗着长，这刘榆也三十年了一直和他大拗劲。他大说，今日太阳出来了，把被子拿出来晒晒，他却去给鸡垒窝。他大说，今年自留地里栽些辣苗吧，他偏种了土豆。

他大活到五十六岁时得了鼓症，临死时想把自己坟修在村后的牛头坡上，棣花的坟地都在牛头坡上，只是花销大，他大说：我死了，别铺张浪费，就埋到河滩的自留地吧。刘榆想，几十年了和大都拗着，这一次得听大一次。他大死后，果然就把大埋在河滩自留地里。第三年，河里发大水，冲了河滩地，刘榆他大的坟也冲没了。

河里原来产一种白条鱼，发大水后新生了昂嗤鱼，之所以是昂嗤鱼，这鱼自呼其名，昂嗤昂嗤叫，像是叹气。

野猫洼村出了个懒人，叫宽心，一辈子没结婚，他死的时候，眼睛都闭上了，嘴还张着，来照料的邻居就看见一股白气从嘴里出来，一溜一溜地从窗格中飘去了。撵出来看，白气没有散，飘到那棵椿树顶上了，成一片云，扇子大的一

interred. However, he was afraid of spending too much, so he insisted: "Don't waste money." Applying some reuerse psychology on his errant son, he added, "Just bury me in our own land on the riverbank." For decades Elm Liu had never listened to his Pa, but in this instance he thought he would comply, even if it was the only time he did. When his Pa passed away, he followed his instructions to the letter and did indeed bury him in their land on the riverbank. The third year after his father's funeral, a flood swept away the grave together with the rest of the bank.

Originally, the river formed the habitat for a kind of fish known as the "sawbelly." After the flood, a new type appeared known as the "rasping catfish." It was so named because of the noise it made. The creature seemed to always be sighing in regret.

Kuanxin was a lazy fellow born in the village of Wild Cat Hollow. He remained a lifelong bachelor. When he died, he eyes closed, but his mouth was still agape. The neighbours who came over to tend to him discovered a stream of white breath emanating from his mouth and drifting out through the lattice in the window. They ran outside to check and found that the mist did not dissipate at all. Rather it floated upwards to the top of the toon tree and morphed into a lump of cloud as big as a fan before hovering away to the west.

As if absorbed in meditation the cloud paused the moment it reached Western Street Village. The sunlight cast the shadow of the cloud onto the roof of Old Tian's house, but hurried on again. Later, it traversed the whole of Rear Tableland Village, Gong Family Bend, and

片，往西再飘。

云飘到西街村，好像停了一下，像思考的样子，阳光将云的影子投在老田家的屋顶上，但很快又走了，经过了后塬村，又经过了巩家湾，最后在崖底村葛火镰家的院子上空不动了。

葛火镰家养着一头公猪，种猪专门给棣花所有的母猪配种的，这一天正好骆驼项村的陆星星拉了母猪来配，云的影子就罩在母猪身上，白猪变成了黑猪。陆星星往天上一看，一片云像个手帕掉下来，他还下意识地躲了一下身子，似乎那云要砸着他，但云没砸着他，而且什么也没有了，他就把母猪牵回了家。

母猪后来生崽，往常母猪一生一窝崽，这回只生了一个崽。这崽样子还可爱，就是不好生长，已经半年了，又瘦又小，与猫常在一处玩。陆星星说：你是猪呀你不长？！它还是不长，到了年底，仅仅四五十斤，还生了一身红茸毛。

finally stopped in motionless suspension above Flint Ge's courtyard in Foot-of-the-Cliff Village ….

Flint Ge kept a boar, set aside for impregnating all the sows of Dihua. On that day, it so happened that Starry Lu was lugging a female pig from Camel Hump Village to cross-bred with him. The shadow of the cloud occluded the body of the sow, turning it from white to black. Starry Lu looked up at the sky. A shred of cloud dropped down like a handkerchief. Unconcsciously, he recoiled from it as if it were about to brain him. This was not to be. Relieved, he drove the pig back home.

Usually the sow would deliver an entire litter of piglets, yet this time only one popped out. The baby appeared sweet, though didn't grow as it should have done. Half a year past and it remained tiny and slender, always wanting to jostle playfully around with the cat. Starry Lu said: "You are a piggy, why don't you get bigger?" The swine still showed no sign of maturing. By the end of the year, it weighed only 40 or 50 pounds. What is more, red bristles covered its entire body.

The following spring, swine fever swept through Dihua, claiming the lives of eight pigs, including this one. When it was breathing its last, Starry Lu noticed a stream of white breath emanating from its maw and floating skywards where it consolidated into a cloud. This time, the cloud was smaller, measuring no larger than a man's palm.

As the cloud travelled over North Canal Village, a stroke of breeze whipped up, pushing it towards the south and Wild Cat Hollow. In the reed flats of the Hollow, wadding was wafting about and became

第二年春上,棣花流行猪瘟,死了八头猪,其中就有这头猪。猪死时,陆星星也发现有一股白气从猪嘴里溜出来,往空里飘了。在空里成了一片云,这云片更小,只有手掌大。

云飘过北渠村上空,起了一阵小风,云就往南飘,又飘回野猫洼村。野猫洼村的芦苇园也飘芦絮,云和芦絮搅在一起,分不清是一疙瘩芦絮还是云,末了,一只蜂落在丁香树的花瓣上,芦絮就挂在树枝上,而云却没了。

丁香花谢后生了籽,籽落在地上的土缝里,来年生出一棵小丁香树。这小树长了两年还是个苗子,放牛的时候,牛把苗子连根拔出来嚼了。苗子一拔出来,又有一丝白气飘了,但在空中始终没有变成云,铜钱大的一团白气。白气移过了院墙,院墙外的水渠沟里有许多蚊子,后来就多了一只蚊子。

这蚊子能飞了,有一夜飞到打麦场上,那里睡了乘凉的人,蚊子去叮人腿,啪地挨了一掌,就掌死了,再没有云,

intermingled with the cloud so that onlookers could not distinguish one from the other. In the end, a bee landed on a lilac bud, the fluffy matter became caught in the branches of a tree and the cloud disappeared.

When the lilac withered and broke into seed, the seeds trickled into the crevices of the ground. The next year, a lilac sapling sprang up, which in its second year was still no taller. The grazing cattle tugged it out at the root and proceeded to chew away. As soon as the lilac was uprooted, a stream of white breath emanated from the earth. This time, it didn't gather into a cloud. Instead, it clumped into a coin-sized gasp. Gliding over the courtyard wall, it reached the mosquito-infested dykes. One more mosquito materialised.

On finding its wings, this mosquito zoomed over to the threshing ground that evening. There the ranks of the sweltering were slumbering and relishing the cool. The insect set about nipping them on the legs and with a swat of the palm wound up squashed. No cloud appeared; not even a wisp of white breath.

As a matter of fact, Lei Family Slope was home to no one of that name. There were two sizeable clans – one named Yu and the other Tian. The Tians were all stumpy-legged and thick-necked. The Yus towered in height and had pinched faces. In spite of this, men outnumbered women in the former family and vice versa, giving the Tians family the whip hand in the village.

A coal mine was located in Luonan County, 50 *li* to the north of Dihua. In the early years of the colliery, a man from the Tian clan

连一点白气都没有。

雷家坡村其实没有姓雷的,是两大族姓,一个姓雨,一个姓田。姓田的都腿短脖子粗,姓雨的高个窄脸,但姓田的男人多,姓雨的女人多,姓田的就控制着村子。

棣花北五十里地的洛南县有煤窑,早年姓田的一个男子在那里当矿工,后来承包了一个煤窑,逐渐做大,成了有钱的老板,便把村里的姓田的男人都带去挖煤,姓田的人家就过上了好日子。姓雨的人家还穷着,女人们就只好到棣花的保姆培训班上报名,她们长得好看,性情也柔顺,培训完后西安的保姆中介公司挑去了七八个,全送去了一些高级领导干部的家里。

二年春节,挖煤的回来了,都有钱,先集体在县上住了一晚宾馆才回村,而那些保姆没有回来,姓雨的说挖煤的在县宾馆住了一夜,吃肉喝酒,还招了妓女,离开后,妓女尿了三天黑水。

went there to dig and rose to be a contractor at one of the pits. As his earnings multiplied, he became a well-to-do boss. He then brought over all his male relatives to join the excavation, allowing everyone a stake in this better livelihood. The members of the Yu family continued to be downtrodden, so the womenfolk headed to Dihua to train as home-helps. Both in appearance and temperament each one of them could be judged as fine. After the course was completed, seven or eight of them were selected by the domestic agency in Xi'an. They were all assigned to the households of senior cadres.

The next spring, the coal miners returned with their pockets stuffed full. Before they reached the village, the team spent a night in a hotel in the county town. The home-helps didn't come back. The gossip among the Yu family had it that the miners were gorging on meat and knocking back liquor in the hotel. They even, it was rumoured, hired the services of call-girls. After they left, the hookers spouted black piss for three days.

When the Spring Festival was over, the men of the Tian family resumed their digging. On the 24th January according to the Lunar Calendar, a fire damp explosion tore through the pit, leaving no survivors. It was on that same day that the seven or eight home-helps arrived back in the village. They informed the villagers that they had flown with their employers to Beijing or Guangzhou. The planes had bogs inside and the crap and piss was all sucked downwards and was vanished into the air.

On 8th April every year, people in Dihua would stage a traditional

春节一过，姓田的男人又去了煤窑，正月二十四那天，井下瓦斯爆炸，没有一个活着出来。也就在这天，七八个保姆回到了村里，她们给村里人说，都曾经跟着主人去过广州或北京，坐的飞机，飞机上有厕所，拉屎尿尿就漏在空中，在空中什么都没有了。

每年四月初八棣花的庙会上要耍社火，中街村准备两台芯子，一台是走兽和地狱，一台是飞禽和天堂，正做着，有人担心这是暗喻雷家坡村，会惹是非，后来就取消了。

药树梁村在棣花的西北角，除了独独一棵大药树外，坡上枣树很多，枣树每一年都有被雷击的。被雷击过的枣木有灵性，县城关镇的阴阳先生曾来寻找雷击枣木做法器，而药树梁村的人出来口袋里也都有枣木刻成的小棒槌，说能辟邪护身。

在三年前夏天，有良在坡上放牛，天上又响炸雷，有良赶着牛就下坡，雷这回没击枣树，把有良击了，但没有击死，脊背上有了一片文字。说是文字，又不是文字，棣花小

New Year carnival with masks and acrobatics. Middle Street Village prepared two main floats. One depicted hell and showcased devils and running beasts. The other depicted flying birds and paradise. During the rehearsal, some folks worried that it might prove an ill omen and the harbinger of trouble for Lei Family Slope, so the event was cancelled.

Cashew Tree Village was situated at the northwest corner of Dihua. Apart from a single huge cashew tree, the slope was awash with dates. Each year, a few of the dates would be felled by thunder. Those thunder-spliced dates possessed a kind of soul. The *yin-yang* master from the county town came there to search for such timber to fashion it into instruments of divination. When the villagers went out, they would all carry a small club hewn from date wood secreted in their pockets. It was purported that they could drive away malevolent entities and safe-guard their beings.

One summer day three years ago, Youliang was grazing his cow on the slope. A peal of thunder ripped through the sky. He drove his cow down the slope. This time the thunder targeted him rather than the dates. He survived and yet some hieroglyphs erupted in the skin on his back. These might have been Chinese characters, but the teachers in Dihua primary school were at a loss as to how to read them. The eighteen signs were divided into three rows. In spite of seeming red as though scratched by fingernails, they neither felt itchy nor painful.

By the end of that autumn, Youliang had been struck down by a creeping paralysis. His hands and feet shrank, leaving him helpless. He

学的老师也认不清。那是十八个像字的字,分三行,发红,像被手抓出的,却不疼不痒。

有良在当年的秋末瘫了,手脚收缩,做不了活,吃饭行走也不行了,整天清坐在家里的藤椅上,让端吃送喝。但有良知道啥时刮风下雨,有一天太阳红红的,他说一会有冰雹哩,谁也不信,但一锅旱烟没吃完,冰雹就噼里啪啦下来了。

还有一回,已在半夜里,有良叫醒家人,说天上掉石头啊,快到院里去。家人知道他说话应,都起来到院子里,一直坐到天亮没有什么石头,才要回屋时,突然天空一团火光,咚的一声,有东西砸在屋顶。过了一会进去看了,屋地上果然有一块石头,把屋顶砸了个洞,地上也一个坑。

西街村的韩十三梦多,一入睡就做梦,醒来又能记清梦的事。他三岁时梦到的都是他成了个老头,胡子又白又长,常拿了一把木剑到一个高墙上去舞。他把梦说给旁人,人都笑他:高墙上能舞剑?但觉得他每天都做梦,梦醒了又给人

could not even feed himself, let alone walk unaided. All he could do was sit at home alone all day long on his bamboo chair, being waited on with food and drink by others. Even so, Youliang now had the gift to discern when wind and rain were apporaoching. One day, the sun shone crimson, but he maintained that there would be hailstones. Nobody believed him. Anyhow, before his neighbours had time to finish a pipeful of tobacco, balls of ice were hurtling down with a *pah-pi-pah-pah*.

Once in the middle of the night, Youliang woke up his family and told them that stones were about to fall from the sky so they should hurry out to the courtyard. They trusted that his prediction would come true, so sat outdoors until daybreak. Still no stones came. As they were about to head inside, a blaze flashed overhead and something thudded against the roof with a *pu-tong* sound. After a while, they went in to inspect. As foretold, a shard of stone lay in a crater in the ground, having torn through the roof.

Thirteenth Han in West Street Village was a dreamer. The second he nodded off, he began to dream and then when he awoke the contents would flood back ever so clearly. At the age of three, he dreamed about turning into an old man with a shaggy white beard. Wielding a wooden sword, the chap would head for the high wall to perform a reel. On hearing his account, others snorted at him: "How could you sword-dance on a high wall?" Nonetheless, people found it humorous that he could dream each and every day and then have perfect recall. Whenever they ran into him, they would ask: "Little fella, what did you dream of this

说梦，很好玩的，见了便问：碎仔，又做啥梦了？韩十三就说他在一个地方走，路很长很宽，两边都是房子，房子特别高，一层一层全是玻璃，路上有车，车多得像河水，一个穿白衣裳的人像神婆子一样指手画脚。村人有去过西安的，觉得这像是西安，就又问：那是街道，街上还有啥？韩十三说：路边都是树，树上长星星。

往后，随着年龄增长，韩十三的梦越来越离奇，但全是城里的事。他在小学时，就梦见自己在一家饭店里炒菜，戴很高很高的帽子，他不炒土豆丝，也不炒豆芽，炒的尽是一些长得怪模怪样的鱼和虾。到了中学时，他梦见自己拿着八磅锤、锯，还有刷墙的刷子，他在给人家刷墙时，那女主人送给他一件制服，但也骂过他。

这样的梦做了三年，中学毕业后没有考上大学，就一直在村里劳动，还当过村会计，又烧过砖瓦窑，娶妻生子。梦还在做，梦到了城里，才知道早先梦到人在高墙上舞剑，那墙是城墙，从城墙上能看见不远处的钟楼，钟楼的顶金光闪闪。那时，村里人有去西安打工的，他问：西安有个钟楼吗？回答说有，又问：城墙上能开车吗？回答说能。韩十三

time?" Thirteenth Han replied that he had envisioned he was walking in some place where the road was long and broad. On either side of the road were houses of colossal stature. Each storey was engineered from glass and the cars down below gushed more densely than a river torrent. A man in white was gesturing with his hands and feet like a warlock. A few of the villagers who had been to Xi'an imagined that this must be the city and so they enquired: "If that's one street, what else can you find there?" He explained that trees lined the roadside and every one of them was spangled with stars.

As he grew older, Thirteenth Han's dreams became increasingly esoteric. And yet they all pertained in some way to elements found in the city. In primary school, he had dreamed about manning a wok in a restaurant with a chef's hat on his head. It wasn't sliced potatoes or beansprouts that he was tossing about in the oil. For whatever reason, he was frying peculiar kinds of fish and shrimps. In high school, his slumbering mind was captivated with the image of a mighty hammer and a saw and brush. He was slathering paint against somebody's wall. The lady of the house kindly sent him a uniform, but also cursed him on another occasion.

Such dreams persisted for three years. Since he failed the university entrance exam, he was forced to labour in the village. Once, he even served as the community accountant. He fired bricks and tiles and such like before getting married and having children. His dreams continued. Subsequently, they found him in the city and he understood that the

就决定也去西安打工。

到了西安,西安的一切和他曾经的梦境一样,他甚至对那里已十分熟悉,还去了他当厨师的酒店,酒店门口有两个石狮子,右边的一个石狮子眼睛上涂着红。但是,韩十三初到西安,没有技术也没有资金,他只好去捡破烂。捡破烂第一天就赚了三十元,这让他非常高兴,想着一天赚三十元,十天就是三百元,一个月九百元呀!第二天,他起得很早上街,却被一辆运土渣的卡车撞倒,而司机逃逸,一个小时后才被人发现往医院送,半路上把气断了。

这一年他三十岁。

墓前立了个碑子,上面刻了生于一九七八年,逝于二〇〇〇年。但不久,刻字变了,是生于一九八〇年,逝于二〇四〇年。村人不知道这刻字怎么就变了?

棣花乡政府设在中街村,是一个大院子,新修的高院墙,新换的大铁门,但门卫还是那个旧老汉。老汉姓夜,从

wall he had perceived himself dancing atop was actually the one that encircles the city. From that vantage point, he could spot the shining gilded roof of the not-so-distant bell tower. Around that time, a number of the villagers made the journey to Xi'an seeking after odd jobs. He asked them: "Is there a bell tower in Xi'an?" The answer was affirmative. He then asked: "Can people drive cars on top of the wall?" Again, they replied "yes." Thirteenth Han decided he should follow them to the city.

In Xi'an, he found that every detail of his dreams tallied with the reality. He even felt a degree of familiarity with the cityscape. He found himself in the same restaurant where he had seen himself employed as a cook. Two stone lions flanked the entrance to that establishment. The eyes of the one on the right were painted red. Unfortunately, he soon realised that he had no skills or capital and was reduced to collecting trash on the streets. The first day he did this, he was over the moon to pocket 30 yuan. He calculated that if he repeated this, in ten days he would earn 300 yuan and in one month 900! So the next morning he woke very early and went out to the street. He was duly mown down by a haulage truck. The driver bolted and it was fully an hour before Thirteenth Han was discovered and sent to the hospital. He was DOA.

That year he had in fact turned 30.

An epitaph was set up in front of his tomb, on which was chiselled the words "Born: 1978; Died: 2000." After a while, the inscription changed to "Born: 1980; Died 2040." The villagers could never fathom: how it was that the numbers had come to be altered.

年轻起人叫他不叫老夜,嫌谐音是老爷,就叫他老黑。

老黑从一九五八年就在这里当门卫,那时乡政府叫公社,今年老黑八十岁,眼不花,耳不聋,身体特别好,乡政府还雇他当门卫。棣花的人其实寿命都不长,差不多每个人家都有着遗憾,比如有些人,日子恓惶了几十年,终于孩子大了,又给孩子娶了媳妇,再是扒了旧屋,盖了一院子新房,家里粮食充足,吃喝不愁,说:这下没事了,该享清福呀!可常常是没事了才两年,最多五年,这人就死了。但老黑活到八十岁,还精神成这样,很多人便请教他的健康长寿秘诀,老黑说,他是每个大年三十晚上,包完饺子了,就制定生活计划的。他的生活计划已经制定到一百二十岁,每一岁里要干什么,怎么去干,都一一详细列出。中街药铺的跛子老王看过老黑一百岁那年的计划,过后给人说,老黑这一年的计划是五月份给孙子的孙子结婚,结婚用房得新盖,他要资助三千元。再是把院子里的井重新淘一下,安个电水泵。再就是,那一年应该是乡政府要换届,要来新的乡长了,这是陪过的第四十五位乡政府领导,他力争陪过七十位。

Dihua Township government office was constructed in Middle Street Village. It consisted of a new courtyard with high walls and a newly-wrought iron gate. The doorman was still that old-timer whose surname was Ye. Ever since he was young, no one addressed him as "Old Ye" because that sounded like an expression for "Old Pa." Rather, they called him "Old Blacky."

Old Blacky had been serving as the doorman since 1958. In that era, the township was known as a "commune." Old Blacky was now 80 years old. His eyes no longer bloomed and his ears were stone deaf. Nonetheless, he was still in fair fettle and the township kept him on to mind the entrance. The truth is that natives of Dihua are seldom long-lived. Almost every person has their regrets. For example, there are those who spend decades feeling worried and vexed about the business of raising and marrying off their children. Others tear down their old homes and erect a new one. Now that they have plenty to eat and drink, they have nothing of which to be afraid. They would say: "All is right as rain. Now is the time to enjoy life." Within two years or perhaps at most five, whoever had spoken these words will drop dead. That is the endless pattern. On the other hand, Old Blacky was a high-spirited octogenarian. Many sought after his secret of longevity. He would respond that as soon as he had finished pressing dumplings on New Year's Eve, he would resume in setting out the plan for his future life. To date, he had plotted out what to do until the age of 120. He would list out in detail what must be accomplished in each year hence and precisely

乡政府院子西墙外有一棵老楸树,这树不是乡政府的,是刘反正家的。棣花再没有这么大的树了,黄昏的时候,中街村的人喜欢在树下说闲话,当说到这树活得久,说老黑也活得久,有一个叫宽喜的人,就也学着老黑定计划,计划他也要活过一百岁。

宽喜只活了六十二岁就死了。

而中街村还有一个人,叫牛绳,牛绳的日子艰难,整天说啥时死呀,死了就不泼烦了。他来问老黑:宽喜也心劲大着要长寿,咋就死了,你这计划是不是不中用?老黑说:宽喜是县上干部,退休了没事么,阎王爷哪会让没事干的人还活在世上?定计划是定着做不完的事哩,不是为了活而活的。宽喜想活他活不了,你想死也死不了,因为你上有老下有小,你任务没完成哩你咋死?

这话说过半年,有一天夜里,老黑在院门口坐着,听见楸树咯吱咯吱响,好像在说:唉,走呀,我走呀。

how he would tackle it. Cripple Wang from the Chinese apothecary on the street once caught sight of his plan for his centenary year. Wang told others that in this particular May the grandson of Old Blacky's grandson was scheduled to get married. The nuptials required a new residence, so he would cough up 3,000 yuan. What is more, he would dredge the well in the courtyard and install an electric-powered pump. The other business jotted down for that year was the fresh elections to the township government. A new Head would come into office – the forty-fifth under whom he would have served under. When all told, he would endeavour to see off 70 of them.

Beyond the western wall of the township courtyard, there grew an ancient Manchurian catalpa tree. It didn't belong to the government, but was rather the property of Liu Fanzheng. No tree in Dihua was more statuesque than this. In the dusk, folk from Middle Street Village would assemble to talk beneath its shade. Of course, they would discuss how long it had lived. On top of that, they mentioned how long Old Blacky had been alive. One fellow, named Kuanxi followed his example and began to sketch out his life plan until the age of 100.

Kuanxi expired at the age of only 62.

Another guy by the name of Bull Rope endured a rough life. He always wanted to know when he would die and asserted that when he died his troubles would be at an end. He visited Old Blacky and asked him: "Kuanxi was determined to live to a great age, so how could he kick the bucket? Does this mean that your plan is humbug?" Old Blacky

第二天，刘反正得了脑溢血死了，他儿子伐了楸树给他大做了棺材。

乡政府大院门口从此没了那棵树，而老黑还在，新一任的乡长才来了七天，老黑每晚要给新乡长说着一段棣花的历史。

said: "Kuanxi was a cadre from the county government. He retired and had nothing to do. How could the God of Hell allow such an idler to hang around in this world? People make plans when they have countless things to do. You don't live for the sake of being alive. Kuanxi wanted to carry on, but didn't. You wanted to die, but can't either. You are sandwiched between youth and old age. How can you die without fulfilling what needs to be done?"

One night six months after their conversation, Old Blacky was sitting by the gate. He heard the rustling of the catalpa tree, which seemed to sound like a sigh, then "Oh, ah. Leaving. I'm leaving."

The next day Liu Fanzheng suffered a fatal brain haemorrhage. His son felled the tree and made it into a coffin.

From then on, the tree was gone from the entrance of the township government courtyard. Old Blacky stayed put all the some. The newly-appointed Head had been in his post for only seven days and every evening the doorman would relate to him some vignette from the history of Dihua.

我的故乡是商洛

人人都说故乡好。我也这么说,而且无论在什么时候什么地方,说起商洛,我都是两眼放光。这不仅出自于生命的本能,更是我文学立身的全部。

商洛虽然是山区,站在这里,北京很偏远,上海很偏远。虽然比较贫穷,山和水以及阳光空气却纯净充裕。我总觉得,云是地的呼吸所形成的,人是从地缝里冒出的气。商洛在秦之头、楚之尾,秦岭上空的鸟是丹江里的鱼穿上了羽毛,丹江里的鱼是秦岭上空的脱了羽毛的鸟,它们是天地间最自在的。我就是从这块地里冒出来的一股气,幻变着形态和色彩。所以,我的人生观并不认为人到世上是来受苦的。如果是来受苦的,为什么世上的人口那么多,每一个人活着又不愿死去?人的一生是爱的圆满,起源于父母的做爱,然后在世上受到太阳的光照,水的滋润,食物的供养,而同时

Shangluo is My Homeland

Everybody insists that his homeland is grand. So do I. Whenever and wherever Shangluo is mentioned my eyes always brighten. This arises not only out of instinct, but as a frisson that wells up from the very essence of my literary creation.

Although Shangluo lies in a mountainous region, standing here Beijing feels like a backwater and so does Shanghai. Although comparatively down-at-heels, its mountains, waterways, sunshine, and air are pure, clean, and rich. I always feel that clouds are condensed out of people's breath; human beings are the streams issuing from the crevices of the earth. Shangluo is located at the head of the State of Qin and the tail-end of the State of Chu. The birds above the Qinling Mountains are the plumed fish launching upwards out of the River Dan and the fish of the River Dan are the birds from above the Qinling Mountains divested of their feathers. They are the most unconstrained creatures to be found between the heavens and the earth. I am merely a brook dribbling out of this patch of land, refracting shapes and colour. Thus my view of life surmises that men

The God of the Earth

do not enter into this world to suffer. If men came here to experience tribulation why then are there so many people on the Earth and why is it that every living person is unwilling to die? A man's life is the perfection of love. It originates from the lovemaking of his parents and then basks in the light of the sun, savours the irrigation of water, and imbibes the nourishment provided by food. At the same time mankind expands and evolves. That is why everyone variously has musical, artistic, or literary talent inbred in their nature. Just as a philosopher once said, "When you see a flower and love it, in actual fact the flower loves you even more." Why then do conflict, hurt, jealousy and terror still afflict this world? Is because of the greed engendered by overpopulation? On account of this, we always maintain that when confronted by death the expiring one is ferrying away a virus and a portion of pain with them. In this case, those who continue to live on should be seized with gratitude toward the deceased. I love Shangluo. I find that the mountains, the waterways, the vegetation, the forests, the flying birds and the scurrying animals are all dear to me. The folks here are not fond of becoming officials. Those who set up roadside stalls and those who scrape a living by begging are all decent compatriots. During these dozens of long years whenever the sons and daughters of Shangluo have dropped by to see me in Xi'an I have always received them with fine cigarettes, choice tea, a happy face, and a sincere heart. Never have I dared to be a poor host. When the sons and daughters of Shangluo ask me for a

传播和转化。这也就是之所以每个人的天性里都有音乐、绘画、文学的才情的原因。正如哲人所说，当你看到一朵花而喜爱的时候，其实这朵花更喜欢你。人世上为什么还有争斗、伤害、嫉恨、恐惧，是人来得太多空间太少而产生的贪婪。也基于此，我们常说死亡是死者带走了一份病毒和疼痛，还活着的人应该感激他。我爱商洛，觉得这里的山水草木飞禽走兽没有不可亲的。这里的不爱为官为民摆摊的行乞的又都没有不是好人。在长达数十年的岁月中，商洛人去西安见我，我从来好烟好茶好脸好心地相待，不敢一丝怠慢，商洛人让我办事，我总是满口应允，四蹄跑着尽力而为。至今，我的胃仍然是洋芋糊汤的记忆，我的口音仍然是秦岭南坡的腔调。商洛也爱我，它让我几十年都在写它，它容忍我从各个角度去写它，素材是那么丰富，胸怀是那么宽阔。凡是我有了一点成绩，是商洛最先鼓掌，一旦我受到挫败，是商洛总能给予慰藉。

我是商洛的一棵草木，一块石头，一只鸟，一只兔，一个萝卜，一个红薯，是商洛的品种，是商洛制造。

我在商洛生活了十九年后去的西安，上世纪八十年代我

favour I always pledge my help readily and do my utmost to gird my four limbs. Even today, my stomach still retains the memory of the cracked corn porridge with sliced potatoes. My accent remains that of the southern foothills of the Qinling Mountains. Shangluo likewise cherishes me. She has permitted me write about her for dozens of years. She has tolerated me writing about her from various angles. Her raw materials are so rich and her mind so broad. Whenever I have achieved a speck, Shangluo has been the first to applaud me. Once I have become frustrated, it has always been Shangluo that has offered me solace.

I am but a blade of grass, a tree, a stone, a bird, a rabbit, a carrot, and a sweet potato tuber from Shangluo. I am the seed of Shangluo, germinated in this place.

I went to Xi'an after having lived for nineteen years in Shangluo. Thrice in the 1980s, I toured around every county here, venturing into almost every town and village both large and small. In the dozens of years since then I have still gone back and forth more than ten times every year. Ever since I arrived in Xi'an, I came to better understand and know more about Shangluo from the perspective of Xi'an. Standing on the latitude of Shangluo from start to finish, I observed and ingested more about China. This is the secret of my life and the cipher for my literary career as well.

To date, I have set down more than ten million words. There are the traces and shadows of Shangluo in all of my works. In my

曾三次大规模地游历了各县，几乎走遍了所有大小的村镇，此后的几十年，每年仍十多次往返不断。自从去了西安，有了西安的角度，我更了解和理解了商洛，而始终站在商洛这个点上，去观察和认知着中国。这就是我人生的秘密，也就是我文学的秘密。

至今我写下千万文字，每一部作品里都有商洛的影子和痕迹。早年的《山地笔记》，后来的《商州三录》《浮躁》，再后的《废都》《妊娠》《高老庄》《怀念狼》，以及《秦腔》《高兴》《古炉》《带灯》和《老生》，那都是文学的商洛。其中大大小小的故事，原型有的就是商洛记录，也有原型不是商洛的，但熟悉商洛的人，都能从作品里读到商洛的某地山水物产风俗，人物的神气方言。我已经无法摆脱商洛，如同无法不呼吸一样，如同羊不能没有膻味一样。

凤栖常近日，鹤梦不离云。

我是欣赏荣格的话：文学的根本是表达集体无意识。我

early years, *Notes on the Mountain Area* and later the *Three Notes on Shangzhou* and *Turbulence*, and later still *The Abandoned Capital*, *Pregnancy*, *Old Gao Village*, *Missing Wolves*, as well as *Shaanxi Opera*, *Happy*, *Ancient Kiln*, *Firefly*, and *Lao Sheng* have each formed a facet of literary Shangluo. Certain stories and anecdotes, both large and small, within each have partially had their prototype in Shangluo while others did not. Yet those who are familiar with Shangluo can detect in those works peculiar spots, mountains, materials, local customs, characters, and dialect expressions which embody the spirit and air of the place. I cannot rid myself of Shangluo, just as I am unable to stop breathing. To put it another way, I am like a sheep that cannot cast off its odour.

A phoenix tower always approaches the sun,

A crane's dream always features the clouds.

I genuinely appreciate Carl Jung's sentiments: "The essence of literature is to express the collective unconsciousness." Moreover, I cleave to these four words: "Robust life without ending." The most difficult and most daunting task in my writing career has been to find and grasp accurately the collective unconsciousness of life. Still, when faced with primal images and when having to notate these one cannot capture them too familiarly and too slickly. What I feel extremely mindful about and care deeply for is the quest to seek novelty and astringency. Such a pity that I have not exactly prospered on either front.

也欣赏"生生不息"这四个字。如果在生活里寻找到、能准确抓住集体无意识,这是我写作中最难最苦最用力的事。而在面对了原始具象,要把它写出来时,不能写得太熟太滑,如何求生求涩,这又是我万般警觉和小心的事。遗憾的是这两个方面我都做得不好。

人的一生实在是太短了,干不了几件事。当我选择了写作,就退化了别的生存功能,虽不敢懈怠,但自知器格简陋,才质单薄,无法达到我向往的境界,无法完成我追求的作品。别人或许是在建造故宅,我只是经营农家四合院。

我在书房悬挂了一块匾:待星可披。意思是什么时候星光才能照着我啊。而我能做到的就是在屋里安了一尊佛像和一尊土地神,佛法无边,可以惠泽众生,土地神则护守住我那房子和我的灵魂。

Life really is too short. One cannot achieve manifold things. When I chose to write, the other functions of survival withered so I couldn't risk being sluggish or slack. I know that I am simple and shallow in my natural constitution, and deficient in quality and talent, being unable to realize the utopia about which I have been dreaming. I have been unable to bring to fruition the works of my imagination. Others may be erecting an ancient Forbidden City. I am only cobbling together my country compound.

In my study there hangs a scroll which states: "Waiting to be under the canopy of the stars." This poses the question: when will the starlight shine on me? All I can do is to set up an effigy of the Buddha and a totem of the God of the Earth in that room. The Buddha's ability is boundless. He can bestow favour upon all mankind. The God of the Earth can defend my house and protect my soul.

(A speech delivered at the Jia Pingwa Literary Symposium held at the Shangluo College of Higher Education, November 2014).

物

The Objects

丑石

我常常遗憾我家门前的那块丑石呢：它黑黝黝地卧在那里，牛似的模样；谁也不知道是什么时候留在这里的，谁也不去理会它。只是麦收时节，门前摊了麦子，奶奶总是要说：这块丑石，多碍地面哟，多时把它搬走吧。

于是，伯父家盖房子，想以它垒山墙，但苦于它极不规则，没棱角儿，也没平面儿；用錾破开吧，又懒得花那么大力气，因为河滩并不甚远，随便去搞一块回来，哪一块也比它强。房盖起来，压铺台阶，伯父也没有看上它。有一年，来了一个石匠，为我家洗一台磨石，奶奶又说：用这块丑石吧，省得从远处搬动。石匠看了看，摇着头，嫌它石质太细，也不采用。

它不像汉白玉那样地细腻，可以凿下刻字雕花，也不

An Ugly Stone

I always felt regret about the ugly stone that lay in front of our home. Its dark expanse sprawled out with the air of a bovine. Nobody knew when it was left there and nobody took any notice of it. Only when the wheat was being cut and our harvest spread before our house to dry, did Grandma say: "That rock's so unsightly; such a waste of space. Find some time and shift it away."

When my uncle was building a house, he wanted to install it as a gable. He abandoned that plan owing to its irregular shape – with no sharp edges or smooth planes. People were reluctant to try and lift a chisel to it, since they didn't think it worth the energy. On the other hand, the river strand was not far away. Any random rock gathered from there would prove superior to this one. As soon as uncle's home was finished, he deemed it unsuitable for serving as a doorstep. One year, a stonemason visited us and wanted to carve us a grindstone. My grandma said: "Use this beastly lump. No need to haul something from afar." The mason inspected it and shook his head, complaining that the texture was too fine and not workable.

像大青石那样地光滑，可以供来浣纱捶布；它静静地卧在那里，院边的槐荫没有庇覆它，花儿也不再在它身边生长。荒草便繁衍出来，枝蔓上下，慢慢地，竟锈上了绿苔、黑斑。我们这些做孩子的，也讨厌起它来，曾合伙要搬走它，但力气又不足；虽时时咒骂它，嫌弃它，也无可奈何，只好任它留在那里去了。

稍稍能安慰我们的，是在那石上有一个不大不小的坑凹儿，雨天就盛满了水。常常雨过三天了，地上已经干燥，那石凹里水儿还有，鸡儿便去那里渴饮。每每到了十五的夜晚，我们盼着满月出来，就爬到其上，翘望天边；奶奶总是要骂的，害怕我们摔下来。果然那一次就摔了下来，磕破了我的膝盖呢。

人都骂它是丑石，它真是丑得不能再丑的丑石了。

终有一日，村子里来了一个天文学家。他在我家门前路过，突然发现了这块石头，眼光立即就拉直了。他再没有走去，就住了下来；以后又来了好些人，说这是一块陨石，从

An Ugly Stone

It was not as delicate as the white marble of the Han Dynasty, which could be incised with characters or blossoms. Nor was it as smooth as dolerite, which lent itself to both washing silk and pounding laundry. It quietly prostrated itself, being unable to enjoy the fullness of the shade offered by the Chinese scholar tree that stood alongside the house. No flowers bloomed around its margins, only sods of creeping wild grass. Gradually, it became encrusted with moss and dark spots. Even the kids in the neighbourhood began to despise it and once tried to get us to team up and tug it away. Our strength was no match for the rock. So, from time to time we would spew curses at it and vent our dislike. Nonetheless, we were impotent and had to leave it undisturbed.

What gave us a shred of consolation was the knowledge that on its surface it bore a pit that was neither large nor small. On rainy days, this would fill with water. It was often the case that when the rains had stopped for three days and the land lay dry, there was still water in this hole. Chickens might peck refreshment from it. On the fifteenth day of every month, we all expected the full moon to rise. Then we would climb onto the rock and gaze at the distant horizon. Grandma would always scold us for fear that we might tumble off. One time, I did just that and my knee was left badly grazed. People all cursed it as an ugly stone. That it was – hideous beyond reason.

Eventually, one day an astronomer came to our village. Passing by our home, he caught sight of this stone. All at once he

天上落下来已经有二三百年了,是一件了不起的东西。不久便来了车,小心翼翼地将它运走了。

这使我们都很惊奇!这又怪又丑的石头,原来是天上的呢!它补过天,在天上发过热,闪过光,我们的先祖或许仰望过它,它给了他们光明,向往,憧憬;而它落下来了,在污土里,荒草里,一躺就是几百年了?

奶奶说:"真看不出!它那么不一般,却怎么连墙也垒不成,台阶也垒不成呢?"

"它是太丑了。"天文学家说。

"真的,是太丑了。"

"可这正是它的美!"天文学家说,"它是以丑为美的。"

"以丑为美?"

straightened his eyes. He didn't leave, but chose to settle in the community. Later on, others dropped by as well and judged that it was a fragment of meteorite that fell to earth two or three centuries ago. It was an artefact of considerable value. Soon after that, a truck pulled up and they carried it away with great care.

All this caught us unawares. This strange and ugly rock had plummeted down from the heavens! It had once mended a hole in the sky, emitting light and warmth. Our ancestors perhaps stared up at it. It once filled them with brightness, hope and longing. Even so, it broke away and ended up lying among the dirty earth and the wild grass for hundreds of years.

Grandma said: "We didn't know it was so unusual! It was no good for building a wall or a step."

"Because it was too ugly." Was how the astronomer put it.

"Yeah, really too ugly."

"But this is where its beauty lies!" The astronomer noted, "Its ugliness is the source of its beauty."

"Ugliness the source of beauty?"

"Indeed. When ugliness becomes an all-surpassing quality, the end result must be beauty. Simply because it was not an ordinary piece of hard rock, it could not be utilised as a wall or step. It couldn't be carved into a sculpture or used for beating laundry either. It wasn't destined for these menial tasks, so was often jeered at by worldly eyes."

"是的,丑到极处,便是美到极处。正因为它不是一般的顽石,当然不能去做墙,做台阶,不能去雕刻,捶布。它不是做这些玩意儿的,所以常常就遭到一般世俗的讥讽。"

奶奶脸红了,我也脸红了。

我感到自己的可耻,也感到了丑石的伟大;我甚至怨恨它这么多年竟会默默地忍受着一切,而我又立即深深地感到它那种不屈于误解、寂寞的生存的伟大。

Grandma's face became flushed, and so did mine.

I was filled with shame and now come to know for myself the greatness of that ugly stone! I had even begrudged how it lay there silently for so many years and put up with all that befell it. What is more, I at once grasped on a very deep level how it weathered loneliness and never surrendered in the face of such misunderstanding.

一棵小桃树

我常想给我的小桃树写点文章，却没写出一个字来。只是自个儿忏悔，又自个儿安慰，说：我是该给它写点什么了。

今天下雨，早晨起来就淅淅沥沥的，我还高兴地说：春雨今年来得这么早！一边让雨淋湿我的头发，一边还想去田野悠然地踏青呢。那雨却下得大了，而且下了一整天。我闭了柴门，倚窗坐下，看我的小桃树，枝条被风雨摇撼着，花一片片落了，大半陷在泥里，三点两点地在黄水里打着旋儿。它瘦了许多，昨日的容颜全然褪尽了，可怜它太小了，才开了一次花。我再也不忍看了，我万般无奈。唉，往日我多么傲慢，多么矜持，原来也是个孱头。那是好多年前的秋天，我们还是孩子。奶奶从市集回来，带给我们一人一只桃子。她说："吃吧，这是'仙桃'；含着桃核儿做一个

A Little Peach Tree

I have often wanted to write a piece about my little peach tree, but have never got around to doing so. This thought fills me with contrition and I comfort myself by saying: "It is high time I composed something."

It rained today. The patter of raindrops started first thing in the morning. I was glad and murmured: "The spring showers have come so early this year!" As the rain dampened my hair I thought about taking a stroll. But the downpour became heavier and fell torrentially for the whole day. I closed the wooden door and on sitting down by the window, began to gaze at my little peach tree. Its branches were being buffeted by the winds and rains, and the blossoms were shed one by one, most of them becoming stuck in the mud, twirling here and there in the brown water.

The tree appeared far gaunter. Gone entirely was its radiance of yesterday. It was a pity that she was so tiny and only broke into blossom once a year. I couldn't bear to watch it anymore, but sighed and felt helpless. Oh, how haughty and reticent I had been in previous days! To be more accurate, I was a coward.

梦,谁看见桃花开了,就会幸福一生呢。"我们都认真起来,含了桃核爬上床去。我却怎么也不能安睡,想起这甜甜的梦是做不成了,又不甘心不做,就爬起来,将桃核儿埋在院子角落里,想让它在那儿蓄着我的梦。

秋天过去了,又过了一个冬天,孩子自有孩子的快活,我竟将它忘却了。春天的一个早晨,奶奶扫院子,突然发现角落里拱出一点嫩绿儿,便叫道:"这是什么呀?"我才恍然记起了它,它是从土里长出来了。

它长得很委屈,是弯弯头,紧抱着身子的。第二天才舒展开身来,瘦瘦的,黄黄的,似乎一碰便立即会断。大家都笑话它,奶奶也说:"这种桃树是没出息的,多好的种子,长出来,却都是野的,结些毛果子,须得嫁接才行。"我却不大相信,执着地偏要它将来开花结果。因为它长得不是地方,谁也不再理会,惹人费神的倒是那些盆景。爷爷是喜欢服侍花的,在屋里,院里,门道里,摆满了各种各样的花草。春天花市一盛,附近的人多来观赏,爷爷便每天一早喊我们从屋里一盆一盆端出去,天一晚又一盆一盆端进来,却从来不想到我的小桃树。它却默默地长上来了。

One autumn day many years ago when we were still children, Grandma came back from the market with a peach for each of us. "Eat," she insisted. "It's an 'enchanted peach'. Hold the stone in your mouth when you go to sleep and you will have a dream. If peach blossom appears in your dream, then you will be happy for the rest of your life."

Our moods became serious and we went to bed with a stone in place. But I could not drop off. I was worried that I might not have such a sweet reverie, yet did not want to abandon all hope. And so I got up and went across and buried the peach stone in a corner of the yard, believing that any future dream would be kept safely stowed away there.

Autumn passed, another winter too. Every child has their own kind of naïve joy. I even forgot about the business. One spring morning as Grandma was sweeping the yard, she chanced upon a small green shoot in the corner. "What is this?" she cried out.

All of a sudden it all came back to me. A new life was sprouting out of the earth.

The plant grew as though it was the victim of some grievance. Its top was curved over and clasped the stem tightly. The next day it flexed itself so it seemed slender and yellow. The gentlest of touches would be enough to snap it.

Everyone chuckled at it. My grandmother said: "A peach tree like this is good for nothing." Grandma reflected. "The seed was decent, but it's burst out in such a frenzy and won't yield any worthwhile fruit. Grafting is what it needs."

舒服。天氣不好，身子癢了，在樹上蹭蹭真

How Cozy to Solve the Itching against the Tree

However, I refused to accept this and stubbornly maintained that it would indeed blossom and burgeon in the future. After that, nobody took notice of it. The peach was in an awkward dilemma. My folks were more concerned about pot-plants. Grandfather, being fond of flowers, made sure our rooms, courtyards and entrances were lush with blooms and foliage. Each spring when his hobby plants were breaking into bud, many people would come over to savour the sight. Early every morning he would bellow orders for us to move the containers out of the house one by one, and take them back in the evening. My little peach tree never crossed his mind. It grew away silently.

It certainly wasn't tardy, rocketing up two feet in the springtime. I was delighted that it was mine, for this was the progeny of the stone that should have begotten a dream. No doubt, my sisters and brothers who lay down with the pit in their mouth had long forgotten what they dreamt that night. My peach tree stood as an everyday reminder and I could have said that my dream was green and it breaking into blossom would confirm my future happiness.

It was at that point that I went away to study in the city. When I came out from the mountains into the metropolis, it dawned on me how miniscule I was: the world beyond the mountains was so vast and the cityscape so full of sights. From then on, I found mettle in my soul, vowing to study hard, strive on with vigour and have a stellar career after graduation. Our country courtyard and the little peach tree inside left my mind as well.

它长得不慢,一个春天长上两尺来高,我十分高兴了:它是我的,它是我的梦种儿长的。我想我的姐姐弟弟,他们那含着桃核做下的梦,或许早已经忘却了,但我的桃树却使我每天能看见它。我说,我的梦是绿色的,将来开了花,我会幸福呢。

也就在这年里,我到城里上学去了。走出了山,来到城里,我才知道我的渺小:山外的天地这般大,城里的好景这般多。我从此也有了血气方刚的魂魄,学习呀,奋斗呀,一毕业就走上了社会,要轰轰烈烈地干一番事业了,那家乡的土院,那土院里的小桃树,便再没去想了。

但是,我慢慢发现我的幼稚,我的天真。人世原来有人世的大书,我却连第一行文字还读不懂呢。我渐渐地大了,脾性也一天天地坏了,常常一个人坐着发呆。心境似蒙上了一层暮气。就在这时候,奶奶去世了,我连夜从城里回到家,家里等我不及,奶奶已经下葬了。看着满屋的混乱,想着奶奶往日的容颜,不觉眼泪流了下来,对着灵堂哭了一场。黄昏时候,在窗下坐着,一外望,却看见我的小桃树。它还在长着,弯弯的身子,努力撑着枝条,已经有院墙高

But I eventually it dawned on me how naïve and simple I was being. The world of humankind is a huge tome of its own and I couldn't even muddle my way through the opening line of it. As I aged older, my temper worsened and I often found myself sitting in solitude with an overcast mind and an enfeebled mentality.

Duly, my grandmother passed away. Misfortunes never come in isolation. I journeyed back all through the night. Since they had no time to spare they went ahead and buried her before I arrived. On seeing the chaotic state of the house and imagining Grandma's careworn face, I dissolved into tears in the memorial hall.

At dusk, I rested under the window. On raising my head, I spied the peach tree. To my astonishment, it was still alive. Behold, that crooked trunk continued to fight to prop up all of its branches and the peach was now the height of the courtyard wall. How had it managed to survive all these years? Gone were Grandpa's floral displays and pots were piled up against the wall. Still it grew. My younger brother told me: "It ought to have blossomed by now, but the pig snapped it with his snout." To their mind it wasn't rooted in a suitable place, nor was it pleasing to the eye. They wanted to chop it down, but Grandma protested. She tended the tree and kept it watered.

Ah, little peach tree, how could I have forsaken you here and forgotten about you so casually as I went drifting around a foreign land?

Looking at the peach tree, I thought of Grandma, whom I had no opportunity to bid farewell to. I was deeply melancholy, and felt

了。这些年来,它是怎样长上来的呢?爷爷的花市早不陈列了,花盆一垒一垒地堆在墙根,它却长着。弟弟说:那桃树被猪拱过一次,要不早就开花了。他们嫌长得不是地方,又不好看,曾想砍掉它,奶奶却不同意,常常护着,给它浇水。啊,小桃树,我怎么将你搴在这里,而漂流异乡,又漠漠地忘却呢?看着桃树,想起没能再见一面的奶奶,我深深懊丧,对不起奶奶,对不起我的小桃树。如今它开了花,虽然长得弱小,骨朵儿也不见繁,而一夜之间竟全开了呢。可是总嫌我的小桃树没有那"灼灼其华"的盛况。一颗"仙桃"的种子,却开得太白太淡了,那瓣儿单薄得似纸,没有肉的感觉,没有粉红的感觉,像是患了重病的姑娘,苍白的脸,偏又苦涩地笑着。我忍不住几分忧伤,泪珠儿又要下来了。

花幸好并没有立即谢去,就那么一树,孤零零地开在墙角。我每每看着它,却发现从来没有一只蜜蜂、一只蝴蝶飞绕。可怜的小桃树。我不禁有些颤抖了,这花莫不就是我当年要做的梦的精灵么?

雨却这么大地下着,花瓣纷纷零落。我只说有了这场春雨,花会开得更艳,香会蓄得更浓;谁知它却这么命薄,

A Little Peach Tree

remorseful about both my grandmother and my little peach tree.

Weak as it was and sparse of bud, it nevertheless erupted into blossom overnight. Once I went to inspect the oleander blossoms in the foothills of the Zhongnan Mountains. I also enjoyed the nectarines at Mawei Slope. Those flowers were a veritable inferno, but my poor little peach was the seedling of an enchanted stone. Her blossoms were too white with papery thin petals. There was no hint of flesh and blush, just like a sick girl whose pale face nonetheless wears a bitter smile. I could not help coming over a little sad, and shedding a few pearly tears.

It was a relief that the blossom did not fade away. That was the only plant to flower forlornly at the corner of the wall. Whenever I looked at it, I never once saw a bee hovering over to express its affection or a butterfly flapping past it. What a poor little peach tree.

Today I cannot help but shiver a little. Was this flowering plant the spirit of the dream I cherished years ago?

Under the heavy rains, the buds are now being discarded. I thought these spring rains would render the colours more vibrant and intensify the bouquet. But who could have predicted that it would have such a baleful fate? It cannot relish the blessings of the shower; it cannot feel this as a catharsis. It offered its fragmentary petals to the wind and the rain. I cried for my grandmother in my heart.

The rain continues. Hundreds and thousands of times my little peach tree has been bent over and struggled to get up. All the blossoms, now thoroughly saturated, have been cast aside piece by piece. Like a

受不得这么大的福分，片片付给风雨了。我心里喊着我的奶奶。雨还在下着，我的小桃树千百次地俯下身去，又千百次地挣扎起来，一树的花一片、一片，洒落得变成赤裸的了。

就在那俯地的刹那，我突然看见树的顶端，高高的一枝上，竟还保留着一个欲绽的花苞，嫩红的，在风中摇着，却没有掉下去，像风浪里航道上远远的灯塔，闪着时隐时现的光。

我心里稍稍有了些安慰。啊，我的小桃树啊！我该怎么感激你，你到底还有一个花苞呢，明日一早，你会开吗？你开的是灼灼的吗？香香的吗？你那花是会开得美的，而且会孕育出一个桃儿来的。我还叫你是我的梦的精灵，对吗？

swan with its eyes wide open, watching its feathers being plucked out one by one until it is completely naked and withered.

The moment the branch skirts the earth I suddenly discover on the uppermost branch a bud has pulled through. With its tender, yellow and pink hues it shivers in the rain, shaking off all the rainwater from all over its body. Several times, it neary falls off, but does not. It is like a lighthouse among the waves on a navigational route, flashing its tender and red and white beam now and then.

There is little consolation in my heart. Oh, little peach tree, how should I thank you? After all, you have a single surviving bud. Will you break into flower first thing tomorrow? Will your blossoms be rich and colourful? Will it be full of scent? My dear, will you be so spellbinding and bear fruit? Can I still call you the spirit of my dream? Could that be so?

残佛

去泾河里捡玩石,原本是懒散行为,却捡着了一尊佛,一下子庄严得不得了。那时看天,天上是有一朵祥云,方圆数里唯有的那棵树上,安静地歇栖着一只鹰,然后起飞,不知去处。佛是灰颜色的沙质石头所刻,底座两层,中间镂空,上有莲花台。雕刻的精致依稀可见,只是已经没了棱角。这是佛要痛哭的,但佛不痛哭,佛没有了头,也没有了腹,莲台仅存盘起来的一只左脚和一只搭在脚上的右手。那一刻,陈旧的机器在轰隆隆作响,石料场上的传送带将石头传送到粉碎机前,突然这佛石就出现了。佛石并不是金光四射,它被泥沙裹着,模样丑陋,这如同任何伟人独身于闹市里立即就被淹没一样,但这一块石头样子毕竟特别,忍不住抢救下来,佛就如此这般地降临了。

Deformed Buddha

I went to the River Jing to search for characterful stones. Originally, this had been a leisurely pursuit, but when I chanced upon a statue of the Buddha. everything took on an air of solemnity. At that moment, I stared up at the sky and spied a propitious cloud. On the only tree for miles there perched a quiet eagle. Without warning, it suddenly launched into flight and went to who knows where.

The Buddha was carved from a grey sedimentary rock, with two layers to the pediment and a hollowed-out middle. Upon the base was fashioned a lotus seat. The delicate carving was still tangible; only the edges had been worn away. This indicated that the Buddha was about to wail. It remained silent since it had been decapitated and part of the torso snapped away too. On the lotus seat the sole remnants were the left foot, which suggested a cross-legged posture, and the right hand that had been resting upon it. All of a sudden, there was a boom from the ramshackle machine. As the conveyer belt was carrying rocks to the stonebreakers, this stone Buddha materialised unannounced. The statuette did not radiate golden light. Instead it was caked in mud and

我不敢说是我救佛，佛是需要我救的吗？我把佛石清洗干净，抱回来放在家中供奉，着实在一整天里哀叹它的苦难，但第二天就觉悟了，是佛故意经过了传送带，站在了粉碎机的进口，考验我的感觉。我庆幸我的感觉没有迟钝，自信良善未泯，勇气还在。此后日日为它焚香，敬它，也敬了自己。

或说，佛是完美的，此佛残成这样，还算佛吗？人如果没头身，残骸是可恶的，佛残缺了却依然美丽。我看着它的时候，香火袅袅，那头和身似乎在烟雾中幻化而去，而端庄和善的面容就在空中，那低垂的微微含笑的目光在注视着我。"佛，"我说，"佛的手也是佛，佛的脚也是佛。"光明的玻璃粉碎了还是光明的。瞧这一手一脚呀，放在那里是多么安详！

或说，佛毕竟是人心造的佛，更何况这尊佛仅是一块石头。是石头，并不坚硬的沙质石头，但心想事便可成，刻佛的人在刻佛的那一刻就注入了虔诚，而被供奉在庙堂里度众生又赋予了意念，这石头就成了佛。钞票不也仅仅是一张纸吗？但钞票在流通中却威力无穷，可以买来整庄的土地，买

Deformed Buddha

silt, giving it a lugubrious appearance just like any great man who lingers alone in the marketplace and is swallowed up by the crowds. And yet, the shape of the stone was very peculiar, so I felt compelled to rescue it. Hence, the Buddha arrived into the world in this way.

I dare not describe myself as its rescuer. Did the Buddha need me to save him? I rinsed the statuette clean and took it home to revere. For the whole day, I lamented how it must have suffered. The next day, enlightenment touched me. The Buddha had processed along that conveyer belt on purpose, pausing before the mouth of the breaker, so as to test my responses. It was a relief to find that I was not so slow and obtuse. I believed that benevolence still existed in my character and I had pluck. From then on, I burned incense everyday and worshipped both him and myself.

We may say that the Buddha is perfect, but this Buddha was deformed. Could it still be considered a Buddha? A deformed human shell without a body or head is repulsive, yet this deformed Buddha still possessed beauty and grace. As I inspected him, the smoke of the incense drifted slowly upwards. His head and body seemed to have miraculously vanished within the clouds. His dignified and compassionate visage face was suspended in the air. His lowered eyes beamed at me. "Buddha," I said. "The hand of the Buddha is the Buddha himself and so too must be his foot." When iridescent glass is broken it retains its lustre. Observe, how serenely and peacefully his hand and foot rest there!

We may say that in the end event the Buddha is a product of the

Deformed Buddha

Deformed Buddha

human mind. Furthermore, this one was only a lump of stone. It is a piece of rock of the sedimentary sort and not so hard. Where there is a will there is a way. The instant the carver put his chisel to work he infused the rock with a sense of piety. When it was enshrined in the temple, with the motive of delivering all sentient creatures from torment, the stone was transformed into a Buddha. A banknote is only a piece of paper as well, yet it gains power when it enters circulation. The territory of a whole village and a whole city, let alone human life and dignity are there to be purchased.

We may say that since it was a Buddha, the Buddha must be almighty. How could it roll and tumble through the River Jing? Yes, one summer day a flood must have come along. It laid waste to the Buddha's temple. The statuette, together with the bricks, tiles, stone cellar and wooden pillars plunged into the river. The bricks, tiles, stone cellar and wooden pillars were pummelled and sifted into fine sand. Only the stone Buddha survived. That was because it was the Buddha. Please note, the character *jing* in the name of the Jing River ought to carry the same meaning as its homonym *jing* – "to pass through." It was not that the Buddha was incapable of escaping the disaster. Rather, it wanted to pass through the waterway to find out where it should reside. That was how he came into my hands. In the ancient legend of Liu Yi, a gentleman used this very river to carry a message to the Dragon King. Now the Buddha itself had passed along it. The Lady Zhen of the River Luo metamorphosed into a god and faded away in a thread of smoke.

来一座城，买来人的尊严和生命。

或说，那么，既然是佛，佛法无边，为什么会在泾河里冲撞滚磨？对了，是在那一个夏天，山洪暴发，冲毁了佛庙，石佛同庙宇的砖瓦、石条、木柱一齐落入河中，砖瓦、石条、木柱都在滚磨中碎为细沙了，而石佛却留了下来，正因为它是佛！请注意，泾河的"泾"字，应该是"经"，佛并不是难以逃过大难，佛是要经河来寻找它应到的地位，这就是它要寻到我这里来。古老的泾河有过柳毅传书的传说，佛却亲自经河，洛河上的甄氏成神，缥缈一去成云成烟，这佛虽残却又实实在在来我的书屋，我该呼它是"泾佛"了。

我敬奉着这一手一脚的泾佛。

许多人得知我得了一尊泾佛，瞧着皆说古，一定有灵验，便纷纷焚香磕头，祈祷泾佛保佑他发财，赐他以高官，赐他以儿孙，他们生活中缺什么就祈祷什么，甚至那个姓王的邻居在打麻将前也来祈祷自己的手气。我终于明白，泾佛

Deformed as it was, this Buddha came to my study in person. I should address it as "the Buddha of the River Jing."

I worshipped the one-handed and one-footed Buddha with my whole heart.

So many people heard that I owned a stone Buddha recovered from the Jing River. I looked at the Buddha and declared that it was an ancient artefact and must be highly efficacious. They all burned incense and kowtowed before it, praying that the Buddha would bless them with wealth, rank, and fertility. They would pray for whatever it was they lacked in their lives. My neighbour, Mr. Wang, even petitioned for good luck before he went to play *mahjong*. Finally, I realised that the reason why the Buddha had no head and body was because all these hordes had pleaded them away. All mortal persons exhibit the utmost piety in the throes of their deepest selfishness. Could the Buddha not recognise their greed? The Buddha was sure to be conscious of this. It just dealt with their selfishness in his own manner. Facing those grasping acolytes he had only himself to sacrifice. Such is the way of the world.

I consecrated the Buddha in my study and burnt incense every day. I baulked at people's pitiful and brazen behaviour, though never made a wish of my own.

"No," the Buddha intoned in my dream last night. "I am not being treated as a Buddha!" This morning when I got up and poked the incense into its place, I knelt down and clasped my hands together. I said, "Buddha, if this is the case I must make a wish now. Since the

之所以没有了头没有了身，全是被那些虔诚的芸芸众生乞了去的，芸芸众生的最虔诚其实是最自私。佛难道不明白这些人的自私吗？佛一定是知道的，但佛就这么对待着人的自私，它只能牺牲自己而面对着自私的人，这个世界就是如此啊。

我把泾佛供奉在书屋，每日烧香，我厌烦人的可怜和可耻，我并不许愿。

"不，"昨夜里我在梦中，佛却在说，"那我就不是佛了！"今早起来，我终于插上香后，下跪作拜，我说，佛，那我就许愿吧，既然佛作为佛拥有佛的美丽和牺牲，就保佑我灵魂安妥和身躯安宁，作为人活在世上就好好享受人生的一切欢乐和一切痛苦烦恼吧。

人都是忙的，我比别人会更忙，有佛亲近，我想以后我不会怯弱，也不再逃避，美丽地做我的工作。

divine is entitled to own beauty and a sacrificial spirit, let him bless my soul and body so they rest in peace and safety. Bless me as a man of the world to savour all the joys and tribulations of human life."

Men are all busy. I am even busier than others. As long as the Buddha is close by, I shall not become weak and timid in the future. I shall not flee any more, but discharge my duty with aplomb.

溪流

我愈来愈爱着生我养我的土地了。

就像山地里纵纵横横的沟岔一样,就像山地里有着形形色色的花木一样,我一写山,似乎思路就开了,文笔也活了。

甚至觉得,我的生命,我的笔命,就是那山溪哩。虽然在莽莽的山的世界里,它只是那么柔得可怜,细得伤感的一股儿水流。

我常常这么想:天上的雨落在地上,或许会成洪波,但它来自云里;溪是有根的,它凉凉地扎在山峰之下。人都说山是庄严的,几乎是死寂的,其实这是错了。它最有着内涵,最有着活力;那山下一定是有着很大很大的海的,永

Streams

I have grown to cherish more and more the land that nutured me. Just as there are crisscrossing valleys and gulleys in the mountain, there are all manner of flowers and trees on those slopes. When I began to write about these mountains, my train of thought seemed ignited and my writing sprang to life.

I even felt that my own life and the life of my pen were the mountain streams. In the luxuriant mountains, though, these channels are pitifully tender and sentimentally thin. I always think that: the rain in the sky could fall to the ground and whip up the waves of a flood, but instead when they leave the clouds, streams strike roots, roots which plunge into the cold land beneath the mountain. People claim that mountains are solemn, so deadly silent. Actually they are wrong. Streams have the most intricate inner essence and possess the greatest vigour. Underneath the mountains there must sit an immense sea. Its emotions are fermenting away and remain forever restless. The only means for it to exhibit those feelings are through those small brooks.

The Big River Flow by My Boat

远在蕴涵的感情,永远是不安宁,表现着的,恐怕便是这小溪了。

或许,它是从石缝里一滴儿一滴儿渗出来的;或许,是从小草的根下一个泡儿一个泡儿冒出来的。但是,太阳晒不干、黄风刮不跑的。天性是那么晶莹,气息是那么清新;它一出来,便宣告了它的生命,寻着自己的道路要流动了。

正因为寻着自己的道路,它的步伐是艰辛的。然而,它从石板上滑下,便有了自己的铜的韵味的声音;它从石崖上跌

It could be that they ooze out drop by drop from every crevice. Or perhaps they gush from the roots of the minute grass roots one bubble after another. The sunlight is powerless to dry them into oblivion and the yellow wind cannot whip them away. Their nature is so crystalline, their breath so refreshing. The moment they are born, they declare their fate and find their paths to meander along.

Simply because they are seeking after their own paths, their steps are arduous. When they slide down from the slate, they reverberate with a bewitching bronze-like echo. When they hurl themselves off the cliffs, they have the hue of white silk. Swirling around in eddies and ponds, their depths become unfathomable. Gradually they broaden and migrate further afield. They course

落，便有了自己白练般的颜色；它回旋在穴潭之中，便有了自己叵不可测的深沉。它终于慢慢地大起来了，要走更远的道儿；它流过了石川，流过了草地，流过了竹林，它要拜访所有的山岭，叩问每一块石头，有时会突然潜入河床的沙石之下去了呢。于是，轻风给了它的柔情，鲜花给了它的芬芳，竹林给了它的凉绿，那多情的游鱼，那斑斓的卵石，也给它增添了美的色彩。

它在流着，流着。它要流到哪里去呢？我想，山既然给了它的生命，它该是充实的，富有的；或许，它是做一颗露珠儿去滋润花瓣，深入到枝叶里了，使草木的绿素传送；或许，它竟能掀翻一坯污泥，拔脱了一丛腐根呢。那么，让它流去吧，山地这么大，这么复杂，只要它流，它探索，它就有了自己的路子。

我是这么想的，我提醒着我，我鼓励着我，我便将它写成了淡淡的文字，聊作这本小书的小序了。

through rocky passes, inundate grasslands, traverse bamboo groves and visit all the mountains, enquiring about each and every lump of rock. Sometimes they abruptly dive abruptly beneath the sediment of riverbeds. The gentle breeze lends them tenderness, the flowers offer them fragrance, and the bamboo donates its cool green. The avid swimming fish and the kaleidoscopic pebbles add a delectable charm.

They trickle on and on. Where are they going? I think that since it was the mountains which offered them life, they should be rich and substantial. Maybe they will be transformed into morning dew and sprinkle themselves over the buds. Or will they penetrate the depths of the leaves, ferrying along chlorophyll for trees and grasses. Alternatively they could dislodge a bank of sludge or tug away a clump of rotten roots. Then, let them flow. The mountains are both vast and complicated. As long as they surge onwards, exploring, streams will pioneer their own paths.

文竹

离开我的文竹,到这闹闹嚷嚷的城市里采购,差不多是一个月的光景了。一个月里,时间的脚步儿这般踟蹰,竟裹得我走不脱这个城市,夜里都梦着回去,见到了我的文竹。

去年的春上,我去天静山上访友,主人是好花的,植得一院红的白的紫的,然而,我却一下子看定了那里边的这盆文竹了。她那时还小,一个枝儿,一拃来高的样,却微微仄了身去,未醉欲醉的样子,乍醒未醒的样子,我爱怜地扑近去,却舍不得手动,出气儿倒吹得她袅袅拂拂,是纤影儿的巧妙了,是梦幻儿的甜美了。我不禁叫道:"这不是一首诗吗?"主人夸我说得极是,便将她送与我了。从此我得了这仙物,置在我的书案,成为我书房的第五宝了。她果然地好,每天夜里,写作疲倦,我都要对着那文竹坐上片刻,月光是溶溶的,从窗棂里悄没声儿地进来,文竹愈觉得清雅,

Asparagus Fern

Almost a month has past since I left behind my asparagus fern and came to make some purchases in the teeming city. Within the space of one month, the pace of passing time seems to have grown somehow hesitant. Seized with the feeling of being enveloped I cannot extricate myself from this place. At night when I dream, I am transported back and can see again my asparagus fern.

Last spring when I went to visit a friend at Tianjing Mountain, it turned out that my host had a penchant for flowers. His courtyard was awash with red, white and purple. Nonetheless, the first thing that caught my eyes was a potted asparagus fern in among these blooms. At that time, it was still very tender and had only a single stem. Its posture – for whatever reason - was gently slanted as though half-awake and half in a stupor. I drew near to the fern with an attitude of tender pity, but could not bring myself to stroke it. The breath I exhaled caused it to dance gracefully and show off the delicacy of its fine shadow and a dream-like sweetness. I could not refrain from uttering "Is this a paean of poetry?" The host praised me by expressing his agreement before

长长的叶瓣儿呈着阳阴,楚楚地,似乎色调又在变幻……。这时候,我心神俱静,一切杂思邪念荡然无存,心里尽是绿的纯净、绿的充实。一时间,只觉得在这深深的黑夜里,一切都消失了,只有我了;我也要在这深深的夜里化羽而去了呢。

她陪着我,度过了一个春天,经过了一个冬天,她开始发了新芽,抽了新叶,一天天长大起来,已经不是单枝,而是三枝四枝,盈盈地,是一大盆的了。我真不晓得,她是什么精灵儿变的,是来净化人心的吗?是来拯救我灵魂的吗?当我快乐的时候,她将这快乐满盆摇曳,当我烦闷的时候,她将这烦闷淡化得是一片虚影,我就守在她的面前,弄起笔墨,作起我的文章了。人都说我的文章有情有韵,那全是她的,是她流进这字里行间的。啊,她就是这般地美好,在这个世界里,文竹是我的知己,我是再也离不得她了。

然而,我却告别了她,到这闹市里来采购,将她托付养育在隔壁的人家了。

handing over the plant as a gift. From then on, I was the custodian of this sprite and it assumed pride of place on the desk in my study, where it became the "fifth treasure." The fern was indeed a thing of wonder. Every night as I became tired from writing I sat and was transfixed by it for a while. The melting moonlight seeped quietly through the lattice on the window. The fern flourished with grace and delicacy. Its elongated frond shone bright and dark like *yin* and *yang*. The clear and light patina appeared to be undergoing metamorphosis …. At this moment, peace flooded through my heart and soul. All ulterior desires were vanquished. My mind was filled with green purity and contentment. In a split second, I was convinced that everything in the depths of that night had disappeared save for me. I too should sprout wings and flap away into the nocturnal ether.

After escorting me through one winter and one spring, she began to develop new twigs and leaves. Every day the plant grew larger and was no longer a lone stem, but possessed three or four and held the whole container beneath its sumptuous canopy. I genuinely did not know from what kind of sprite she had come from. Did she appear to purify men's minds and to save my soul? When I was happy, she channelled my joy through allowing her every limb to sway. When I was downcast, she would decoct my gloom into lighter shadows. Then, in front of her I began to prepare my ink and pens for creative work. People say that my articles abound in passion and grace. She deserves full credit for this since she meanders through every line I have set down. How

这人家会精心养育吗？他们是些粗心的人，会把她一早端在阳光下晒着，夜来了，会又端着放在室里吗？一天可以办到，两天可以办到，十天八天，一个月，他们会是不耐烦了，把她丢在窗下，随那风儿吹着，尘儿迷着，那叶怕要黄去了，脱去了，一片一片，卷进那猪圈牛棚任六畜糟踏去了。那么，每天浇一次水，恐怕也是做不到的，或许记得了倒一碗半杯残茶，或许就灌一勺涮锅水呢。那文竹怎么受得了呢？她是干不得的，也是湿不得的，夕阳西下的时候，舀一碗水来，那不是净水，也不是溶着化肥的水，是在瓶子里抠了很久的马蹄皮子的水，端起来，点点滴滴地渗下去的呢……

唉，我真糊涂，怎么就托付了他们，使我的文竹受这么大的委屈啊！

采购还没有完成，身儿还不能回去，愁得无奈了，我去跑遍这城的所有花市，去看这里的文竹。文竹倒也不少，但全都没有我的文竹的天然，神韵也淡多了，浅多了。但是，得意扬扬之际，立即便是无穷无尽地思念我的文竹的愁绪。夜里歪在床上，似睡却醒，梦儿便姗姗地又来了，但来到的

phenomenal it was. In this world, the fern was my soulmate. I could no longer tear myself away from her.

Even so, I had to bid farewell to the plant and come to the teeming city. She was left in the care of a neighbouring family.

Would those folks nurture her with care? They are slovenly people. Will they remember to move her into the sunshine in the morning and carry her back into the room in the evening? They might do that for a day or two. As for eight or ten days or even a month, they would probably patience. They might place her under the window, where she would be manhandled by the wind and left daubed with dust. Her leaves would then become withered and fall off one by one, floating out into the pigsty or the cow byre, where they would be ravaged by animals. On the other hand, I fear they might not water her once every day. They could perhaps spare half a bowl of cold tea or dishwater. How could the plant bear this? She needs to be neither too wet nor too dry. When the sun is setting, a bowl of water should be served. The water should not be pure, clean water, nor full of fertiliser. Rather it should have been stored in a bottle for a long time together with the skin from horse hooves. The refreshment should be dribbled in from a height.

I am really at a loss. How could I have entrusted her to them and let my dear plant suffer!

My purchasing is still not finished and I cannot go back. Beset with feeble worry, I head across town to the flower market to see what their ferns are like. Plentiful as these are, none has such a natural grace

不是那文竹，是一个姑娘，我惊异着这女子的娟好，她却仄身伏在门上，抖抖削肩，唧唧嗒嗒地哭泣了。

"你为什么哭了？"我问。

"我伤心，我生下来，人人都爱我，却都不理解我，忌妒我，我怎么不哭呢？"她说，眼泪就流了下来。

哦，这般儿的女子处境，我是知道的：她们都是心性儿天似的清高，命却似纸一般的贱薄，峣峣者易折，皎皎者易污啊。

"他们为什么这样？他们为什么要这样？"

我却淡淡地笑了："谁叫你长得这么美呢？"

她却睁大了眼睛，定定地看着我，有了几分愤怒；我很是窘了。她突然说：

as mine. They are poor and insipid by comparison. Proud as I am of the plant, my mind is swamped with longing for her. At night, I curl up in bed and half asleep I form the impression of her sashaying delicately into my dream. Needless to say, my visitor is not the asparagus fern, but a girl. Her beauty overwhelms me. She leans against the door, her slender shoulders trembling as she sobs.

"Why are you crying?" I ask.

"I am heartbroken. Everyone loved me when I was born but no one understands me. They all envy me, so how can I not cry?" Tears trickle down from her eyes.

Oh! I understand the plight of girls like her. Their temperament is as noble as the sky, but their fate is as humble as a scrap of paper – easily torn up, yet glistening white and ready to be soiled.

"Why do they treat me in this way? Why do they treat me in this way?"

I smile gently: "How come you were born so pretty?"

With her eyes wide open, she stares lividly at me. I become very embarrassed. She suddenly blurts out:

"Is it my fault? I came into this world and this seems to have been my role – showing off my looks. Maybe I am fragile and weak. In spite of it all I am delicate and noble. I am headstrong and won't stand for being messed over."

I am taken aback.

"Who are you and what is your name?"

"美是我的错吗?我到这个世上来,就是来作用、贡献美的。或许我是纤弱的,但我娇贵,但我任性,我不容忍任何污染!"

我大大地吃惊了:

"你是谁,叫什么名字?"

"文竹!"

文竹?我大叫一声,睁开眼来,才知道是一场梦了。啊,是一场梦呢?往日的梦醒,使我失落,这梦,却使我这般地内疚,这般地伤感!我沉吟着,感到我托付不妥的罪过,感到我应该去保护我的责任,我一定是要回去的了,我得去看我的文竹了。

"Asparagus Fern"

"Asparagus Fern?" With a loud cry I open my eyes and realise that it is a dream. Oh! It is just a dream. In the past my dreams always left me feeling perplexed when I woke up. This one, however, touchs me with guilt and sadness. In this silence I meditated as a reprobate. I must do my duty. I must go back and be reunited with my asparagus fern.

陶俑

秦兵马俑出土以后,我在京城不止一次见到有人指着在京工作的陕籍乡党说:瞧,你长得和兵马俑一模一样!话说得也对,一方水土养一方人,一方人在相貌上的衍变是极其缓慢的。我是陕西人,又一直生活在陕西,我知道陕西在西北,地高风寒,人又多食面食,长得腰粗膀圆,脸宽而肉厚,但眼前过来过去的面孔,熟视无睹了,倒也弄不清陕西人长得还有什么特点。史书上说,陕西人'多刚多蠢',刚到什么样,又蠢到什么样,这可能是对陕西的男人而言,而现今陕西是公认的国内几个产美女的地方之一。朝朝代代里陕西人都是些什么形状呢,先人没有照片可查,我只有到博物馆去看陶俑。

最早的陶俑仅仅是一个人头,像是一件器皿的盖子,它两眼望空,嘴巴微张。这是史前的陕西人。陕人至今没有

Pottery Figures

After the Qin Terracotta Army was unearthed, I more than once observed people pointing at Shaanxi folk working in Beijing and saying: "Look! You are just like the terracotta warriors. Alike as two peas in a pod!" What they said is quite correct. Man is indeed the product of his environment. His appearance evolves incrementally over time. I am a native and long-term resident of Shaanxi. Of course, Shaanxi is to be found in the northwest of China where the land is steep and the winds bracing. Locals love to eat food made from wheat flour. They are stout-waisted, with broad shoulders, wide faces and brawny bodies. As people file before me, I cast a blind eye upon what is so familiar to me. I do not have a firm idea about what other physical characteristics Shaanxi folk share. According to historical records, Shaanxi folk are "strong-willed and simple-minded." This strength and simplicity likely refers to Shaanxi males. Nowadays, this province is loudly acclaimed all over China for being able to produce beauties. What were the physical attributes of Shaanxi people in dynasties gone by? We have no photographs of our ancestors, so I must turn to study the pottery figures on display in the

小眼睛，恐怕就缘于此，嘴巴微张是他们发明了陶埙，发动起了沉沉的土声。微张是多么好，它宣告人类已经认识到自己在这个世界上的位置，它什么都知道了，却不夸夸其谈。陕西人鄙夷花言巧语，如今了，还听不得南方"鸟"语，骂北京人的"京油子"，骂天津人的"卫嘴子"。

到了秦，就是兵马俑了。兵马俑的威武壮观已妇孺皆晓，马俑的高大与真马不差上下，这些兵俑一定也是以当时人的高度而塑的，那么，陕西的先人是多么高大！但兵俑几乎都腰长腿短，这令我难堪，却想想，或许这样更宜于作战。古书上说"狼虎之秦"，虎的腿就是矮的，若长一双鹭鸶腿，那便去做舞伎了。陕西人的好武真是有传统，而善武者沉默又是陕西人善武的一大特点。兵俑的面部表情都平和，甚至近于木讷，这多半是古书上讲的愚，但忍无可忍了，六国如何被扫平，陕西人的爆发力即所说的刚，就可想而知了。

秦时的男人如此，女人呢？跽坐的俑使我们看到高髻后挽，面目清秀，双手放膝，沉着安静，这些俑初出土时被

museum.

The earliest surviving work of figurative pottery consists of only the head of a man. Resembling the lid of some lost container, its eyes gaze up at the sky, its mouth opened imperceptibly. This is a prehistoric Shaanxi person. In the present day, we do not have tiny eyes. This discrepancy can be traced back to this object. Its mouth is opened slightly because that was the age in which the clay ocarina was invented. They wanted to channel the gravid sound of the earth. How wonderful it is that their mouths were slightly opened. This declares that human beings had already realised their place in this world. They knew everything, but never boasted. Shaanxi folk look down upon the silver-tongued. Up until now, they are still loath to listen to the "twittering" of southerners, the "greasy lips" of Beijingers and the "slippery tongues" of Tianjin.

When the Great Qin Dynasty was established, the Terracotta Army was cast. Young and old, male and female alike, all know of the might and grandeur of the earthenware warriors. The pottery horses are almost life-sized and the human figures were surely modelled to scale. How great, then, were the ancestors of Shaanxi people. However, what makes me feel embarrassed is that the warriors have elongated midribs and stumpy legs. On second thoughts, this may have rendered them better adapted to the conditions of ancient warfare. The history books record that "The Great Qin had an army of wolves and tigers." Tigers' legs are short. If they had the legs of an egret, they would only be able to become kabuki dancers. Shaanxi people have the tradition of loving martial arts. One of their outstanding characteristics is that those who excell at this

认作女俑，但随着大量出土了的同类型的俑，且一人一马同穴而葬，又唇有胡须，方知这也是男俑，身份是在阴间为皇室养马的"圉人"。哦，做马夫的男人能如此清秀，便可知做女人的容貌姣好了。女人没有被塑成俑，是秦男人瞧不起女人还是秦男人不愿女人做这类艰苦工作，不可得知。如今南方女人不愿嫁陕西男人，嫌不会做饭、洗衣、裁缝和哄孩子，而陕西男人又臭骂南方男人竟让女人去赤脚插秧，田埂挑粪，谁是谁非谁说得清？

汉代的俑就多了，抱盾俑，扁身俑，兵马俑。俑多的年代是文明的年代，因为被殉葬的活人少了。抱盾俑和扁身俑都是极其瘦的，或坐或立，姿容恬静，仪态端庄，服饰淡雅，面目秀丽，有一种含蓄内向的阴柔之美。中国历史上最强盛的为汉唐，而汉初却是休养生息的岁月，一切都要平平静静过日子了，那时的先人是讲究实际的，俭朴的，不事虚张而奋斗的。陕西人力量要爆发时，那是图穷匕首见的，而蓄力的时候，则是长距离的较劲。汉时民间雕刻有"汉八刀"之说，简约是出名的，茂陵的石雕就是一例，而今，陕西人的大气，不仅表现在建筑、服饰、饮食、工艺上，接人待物言谈举止莫不如此。犹犹豫豫，瞻

skill always keep it to themselves. The facial expressions of these pottery figures seem calm, almost clumsy. This could be what the history books meant by "simple-minded." When their patience was pushed to the limits, they rose up and conquered the six rival states. From how these forces sprang into action, people can well imagine too what the "strong will" mentioned in the annals was.

These descriptions refer to Shaanxi males at the time of the Qin Dynasty. What about Shaanxi women? Those kneeling terracotta warriors each have their hair bound into a knot at the back of their heads. Their faces are delicate and comely and the way their hands are pressed against the knees conveys an attitude of calmness and quiet. When they were first excavated, these were regarded as "she-warriors." As more warriors of this type were unearthed, it was discovered that each of them shared a burial pit with a steed. Furthermore, they sported moustaches. Then it became obvious that these were men as well – stabl-ehands who were to take charge of the emperor's horses in the underworld. Oh, if a stable-hand could look like this, you can only imagine how pretty the women would have be at this time! There are no pottery figurines of females. Was that because Qin men were chauvinists or were they unwilling to set their womenfolk to toil? Nobody knows. Nowadays, women from the South are not disposed towards marrying Shaanxi men. They complain that Shaanxi men cannot cook, or launder or tailor clothes. They are even incapable of minding their own children. Whereas, Shaanxi men will curse men in the South because they set their women to work barefoot, planting out rice seedlings in the paddy and hauling manure along the field terraces. Whoever has the right idea, no

前顾后，不是陕西人性格，婆婆妈妈，鸡零狗碎，为陕西人所不为。他不如你的时候，你怎么说他，他也不吭，你以为他是泼地的水提不起来了，那你就错了，他入水瞄着的是出水。

汉兵马俑出土最多，仅从咸阳杨家湾的一座墓里就挖出三千人马。这些兵马俑的规模和体型比秦兵马俑小，可骑兵所占的比例竟达百分之四十。汉时的陕西人是善骑的。可惜的是现在马几乎绝迹，陕西人自然少了一份矫健和潇洒。

陕西人并不是纯汉种的，这从秦开始血统就乱了，至后年年岁岁的抵抗游牧民族，但游牧民族的血液和文化越发杂混了我们的先人。魏晋南北朝的陶俑多是武士，武士里相当一部分是胡人。那些骑马号角俑、舂米俑，甚至有着人面的镇墓兽，细细看去，有高鼻深目者，有宽脸彪悍者，有眉清目秀者，也有饰"魋髻"的滇蜀人形象。史书上讲过"五胡乱华"，实际上乱的是陕西。人种的改良，使陕西人体格健壮，易于容纳，也不善工计，易于上当受骗。至今陕西人购衣，不大从上海一带进货，出门不愿与

one can judge.

In the Han Dynasty, more warriors appeared. There were warriors who clutched shields in their hands, figures modelled from sideways on, and warriors with horses. The abundance of earthenware replicas signifies that this was a civilised era since it suggests that fewer bond-slaves were being buried alive with their masters. The figures with shields and a sideways aspect are all very thin. Some are seated and others are standing up. They are serene in their appearance, poised in their manner, plain and delicate in dress, and wear friendly expressions – the embodiment of feminine tenderness. The Han and Tang Dynasties were the most powerful periods in Chinese history. The beginning of the Han Dynasty marked a period of rehabilitation. Everything went on peacefully. Our ancestors at that time focused on practical and simple living. They strove on without ostentation. When the strong will of Shaanxi people exploded, it was like a long scroll being unfurled to reveal a dagger at the very end. But when they cultivated their power it was like a marathon race. Among the folk sculpture of the Han Dynasty, "eight cut" carvings were especially renowned. Their simplicity was well-known, with the benchmark being the stonework at the Maoling Mausoleum. These days, the sublimity of Shaanxi is displayed not only in architecture, clothing, food, and handicrafts, but also in their everyday speech and etiquette. Shaanxi folk are not by nature hesitant or overcautious. They dislike a fuss being made over trivial matters and when they find themselves on a backfoot they will keep silent no matter how they are lambasted. You may think that they are like the water sprayed out over the land, which can never be retrieved, but you are wrong. The irrigation percolates

Woman and Pottery

through the soil with every intention of spurting forth again in the future.

The lion's share of warriors and horses has been dug out of the tombs of the Han Dynasty. Three thousand were found in a single tomb at Yangjiawan in Xianyang. Their size and scale are smaller than those of the Qin. Even so, cavalrymen make up forty percent of the troops. In the Han Dynasty, Shaanxi people were adept equestrians. It is a pity that even the horse has almost become extinct. Naturally, therefore, local people lack a streak of unrestrained grace and robustness. To this day, Shaanxi people seldom buy clothes from Shanghai and and are unwilling to travel in the company of those from the South.

Shaanxi people are not of purebred Han stock. From the Qin Dynasty, their blood became diluted. Year in, year out, they engaged in battle with the nomadic peoples. And yet the blood and culutre of our ancestors intermingled still further with those of the nomads. Many military soldiers feature among the pottery figures of the Wei and Jin and the Northern and Southern Dynasties. A number of these are of the Hun race. If you observe closely, the riders who carry a bugle, the warriors who pound rice and even the human-faced tomb-guarding animals are all large-nosed with deep-set eyes. Some of them are doughty and have a wide face. Others appear handsome, with neat eyebrows and there are those who even sport the hairstyles of Yunnan and Sichuan people. History books mention that "five nomadic tribes disturbed China," when in fact they disturbed only Shaanxi. Owing to their prodigious hybridisation the folks of Shaanxi seem robust and powerful in build, tolerant in nature and easy to be cheated, while never cheating

南方人为伴。

正是有了南北朝的人种改良,隋至唐初,国家再次兴盛,这就有了唐中期的繁荣,我们看到了我们先人的辉煌——

天王俑:且不管天王的形象多么威武,仅天王脚下的小鬼也非等闲之辈,它没有因被踩于脚下而沮丧,反而跃跃欲试竭力抗争。这就想起当今陕西人,有那一类,与人抗争,明明不是对手,被打得满头满脸的血了却还往前扑。

三彩女侍俑:面如满月,腰际浑圆,腰以下逐渐变细,加上曳地长裙构成的大面积的竖线条,一点也不显得胖或臃肿,倒更为曲线变化的优美体态。身体健壮,精神饱满,以力量为美,这是那时的时尚。当今陕西女人,两种现象并存,要么冷静、内向、文雅,要么热烈、外向、放恣,恐怕这正是汉与唐的遗风。

others. .

Owing to the hybridisation in the Southern and Northern Dynasties, from the Sui Dynasty to the beginning of the Tang Dynasty, China regained its prosperity. Hence, the golden age in the middle Tang Dynasty through which we can witness the glory of our ancestors.

* * *

Apart from the mighty and powerful figure of the Heavenly King, the small ghosts underneath his feet are also somewhat unusual. He doesn't become frustrated simply because he is trodden upon. Instead, he is spoiling for a chance at retaliation. This reminds me of the character of present-day Shaanxi people. They are of that sort who clearly knows that they are no match for their rivals, but still lunge forward, their faces and heads bloodied.

* * *

The tricoloured ladies-in-waiting: With full-moon faces and plump waists which taper off moving downwards, their long skirts cascade over the floor causing them not to look fat, but rather to assume a more curvaceous state of beauty. They are healthy in build and vigorous in spirit. It was the trend at that time to assume that power was synonymous with beauty. For Shaanxi women of today, the two phenomena co-exist. On the one hand they remain calm, bashful and full of grace. On the other they are outgoing, warm, and unrestrained. This is perhaps the legacy of the Han and Tang Dynasties.

* * *

Woman on horseback: The "horse" is in fact a zebra; the woman is a paragon with a bared chest and arms. She appears regal and alluring,

骑马女俑：马是斑马，人是丽人，袒胸露臂，雍容高雅，风范犹如十八世纪欧洲的贵妇。

梳妆女坐俑：裙子高系，内穿短襦，外着半袖，三彩服饰绚丽，对镜正贴花黄。随着大量的唐女俑出土，我们看到了女人的发式多达一百四十余种。唐崇尚的不仅是力量型，同时还是表现型。男人都在展示着自己的力量，女人都是展示着自己的美，这是多么自信的时代！

陕西人习武健身的习惯可从一组狩猎骑马俑看到，陕西人的幽默、诙谐可追寻到另一组说唱俑。从那众多的昆仑俑、骑马胡人俑、骑卧驼胡人俑、牵马胡人俑，你就能感受到陕西人的开放、大度、乐于接受外来文化了。而一组塑造在骆驼背上的七位乐手和引吭高歌的女子，使我们明白了陕西的民歌戏曲红遍全国的根本所在。

秦过去了，汉过去了，唐也过去了，国都东迁北移与陕西远去，一个政治经济文化的中心日渐消亡，这成了陕西人最大的不幸。宋代的捧物女绮俑从安康的白家梁出

exuding the air of an aristocratic lady in eighteenth-century Europe.

* * *

Woman seated before a dressing table: Her skirts are rolled up high with her underwear on display. The sleeves of her blouse are turned back and the tricolour dress is strikingly gaudy. Before the looking glass she is pinning a flower into her hair. As more female statuettes have been recovered from tombs, we can observe how back then there were more than 140 different hairstyles. The Tang Dynasty not only worshipped power, but revelled in showing it off. All the men flaunted their power, while all the women showcased their beauty. What a self-confident era they lived in!

* * *

Shaanxi peoples' habit of practicing martial arts and keeping fit can be discerned from a set of hunting warriors on horseback. The humour and jocosity of Shaanxi people is evident from the set of chatting and singing figurines. From the earthenware figures of Kunlun mountain-dwellers, and the Hunnish equestrians, riders of couchant camels and horse minders, we can discern that Shaanxi people are open, broadminded and receptive towards foreign cultures. The other troupe of seven female musicians sings loudly and in high spirits as they balance on the backs of dromedaries. Thus we can tell why Shaanxi folksong and opera have been so popular and widely-performed across China.

* * *

The Qin Dynasty is gone; the Han Dynasty has passed by; the Tang Dynasty has ended as well. The capital of the nation has migrated northwards and eastwards, further away from this province. In turn, the

土,她们文雅清瘦,穿着"背子"。还有"三搭头"的男俑。宋代再也没有豪华和自信了,而到了明朝,陶俑虽然一次可以出土三百余件,仪仗和执事队场面壮观,但其精气神已经殆失,看到了那一份顺服与无奈。如果说,陕西人性格中有某些缺陷,呆滞呀,死板呀,按部就班呀,也都是明清精神的侵蚀。

每每浏览了陕西历史博物馆的陶俑,陕西先人也一代一代走过,各个时期的审美时尚不同,意识形态多异,陕西人的形貌和秉性也在复复杂杂中呈现和完成。俑的发生、发展至衰落,是陕西人的幸与不幸,也是两千多年的中国历史的幸与不幸。陕西作为中国历史的缩影,陕西人也最能代表中国人。二十世纪之末,中国实行改革开放政策,地处西北的陕西是比沿海一带落后了许多,经济的落后导致了外地人对陕西人的歧视,我们实在是需要清点我们的来龙去脉,我们有什么,我们缺什么。经济的发展文化的进步,最根本的并不是地理环境而是人的呀,陕西的先人是龙种,龙种的后代绝不会就是跳蚤。当许许多多的外地朋友来到陕西,我最于乐意的是领他们去参观秦兵马俑,去参观汉茂陵石刻,去参观唐壁画,我说:"中

economic, political and cultural centre has waned. This is the matter of greatest pity for Shaanxi people. A pottery likeness of females bearing gifts in their hands has been unearthed from Bai Family Ridge in Ankang. They are delicate and slim, clad in unisex-style overcoats. Male warriors too wear three-piece outfits. In the Song Dynasty, gone was the sense of luxury and self-confidence. Advancing through into the Ming Dynasty, it may be the case that in excess of 300 specimens of ceramic figures are unearthed from a single tomb, Despite the guard of honour and the company of stewards still appear magnificent, though their inner spirit is gone away completely. All we can see now is an obedient and helpless shell. If we say that Shaanxi people have shortcomings in terms of their personalities, such as being clumsy, too frank, and following the letter of the law, this is because of the corrosive effects the Ming and Qing Dynasties had on their collective spirit.

Every time I have been to examine the pottery figures in the Shaanxi History Museum, I feel that I have witnessed the passing of one generation after another of Shaanxi forebears. Each period had its own unique aesthetics and ideology. These complicated vicissitudes also served to nurture the appearance and nature of Shaanxi people have also been nurtured through these complicated vicissitudes. The invention, development and decline of the pottery figures have been a source of simultaneous contentment and unease. For more than two thousand years they have moreover, bequeathed both these emotions to the Chinese nation.

As a microcosm of Chinese history, Shaanxi folk can represent the country as a whole. Starting in the late twentieth century, China

国的历史上秦汉唐为什么强盛,那是因为建都在陕西,陕西人在支撑啊,宋元明清国力衰退,那罪不在陕西人而陕西人却受其害呀。"外地朋友说我言之有理,却不满我说话时那一份红脖子涨脸:瞧你这尊容,倒又是个活秦兵马俑了!

initiated its policy of Reform and Opening-Up to the outside world. Located as it is in the northwest of China, Shaanxi has fallen behind those provinces along the seaboard. Its economic backwardness has given outsiders a pretence to look down upon its inhabitants. We should take stock of what has happened in the past in order to foretell the future. What do we possess and what do we lack? The key ingredient for economic development and cultural renaissance is not the geographical environment, but human beings themselves. The ancestors of Shaanxi people were the seed of the dragon. The offspring of this seed could not turn out to be fleas. When many of my friends have visited this province, my greatest pleasure has been to lead them to the Terracotta Army and to take them to see the stone statues at the Maoling Mausoleum, together with the Tang Dynasty frescoes. I ask them: "In Chinese history why was it that the Qin, the Han and the Tang were so powerful? It's because they built their capitals in Shaanxi. Shaanxi people were their bedrock. The Song, Yuan, Ming and Qing never enjoyed such strong central power. Shaanxi people should not be blamed, but they were harmed in this process too." My friends always concur with my sentiments, but take exception to how I express this, my neck and face flushing red with enthusiasm. They respond: "Take a look in the mirror, a ruddy terracotta warrior has just sprung to life!"

壁画

陕西的黄土厚,有的是大唐的陵墓,仅挖掘的永泰公主的,章怀太子的,懿德太子的,房陵公主的,李寿、李震、李爽、韦洞、章浩的,除了一大批稀世珍宝,三百平方米的壁画就展在博物馆的地下室。这些壁画不同于敦煌,墓主人都是皇戚贵族,生前过什么日子,死后还要过什么日子,壁画多是宫女和骏马。有美女和骏马,想想,这是人生多得意事!

去看这些壁画的那天,馆外极热,进地下室却凉,门一启开,我却怯怯地不敢进去。看古装戏曲,历史人物在台上演动,感觉里古是古,我是我,中间总隔了一层,在地下室从门口往里探望,我却如乡下的小儿,真的偷窥了宫里的事。"美女如云",这是现今描写街上的词,但街上的美女有云一样地多,却没云那样地轻盈和简淡。我们也常说"唐女肥婆",甚至怀疑杨玉环是不是真美?

Wall Paintings

The yellow earth of Shaanxi lies thick. There is an overabundance of tombs from the Great Tang Dynasty. Only a few have been excavated, including those of Princess Yongtai, Prince Zhang Huai, Prince Yide, Princess Fang Ling, Li Shou, Li Zhen Li Shuang, Wei Ying and Zhang Hao. In addition to a great number of rare treasures, more than 300 square metres of tomb frescoes have been discovered, which are now on display in the basement of the Shaanxi History Museum. These murals are different from the specimens in the Dunhuang Grottoes. The occupants of the tombs all belonged to the ranks of royalty or were their kinsmen. They wanted to prolong their noble lives after death. The wall paintings are thus composeed of ladies in waiting and steeds. Imagine if you will: beauties alongside thoroughbreds – what a rich, contented existence they lived and breathed!

The day when I went to visit the murals it was scorching outside, but rather cool in the underground gallery. When the door swung open, I was so timid that I dare not step over the threshold. Whenever we watch ancient costume dramas, the historical figures stalk back and forth across the stage. One feels that history is history and I am who I am. There is always a barrier between the performing space and the audience.

壁画中的宫女个个个头高大，耸鼻长目，丰乳肥臀，长裙曳地，仪表万方，再看那匹匹骏马，屁股滚圆，四腿瘦长刚劲，便得知人与马是统一的。唐的精神是热烈，外向，放恣而大胆的，他的经济繁荣，文化开放，人种混杂，正是现今西欧的情形。我们常常惊羡西欧女人的健美，称之为"大洋马"，殊不知唐人早已如此。女人和马原来是一回事，便可叹唐以后国力衰败，愈是被侵略，愈是向南逃，愈是要封闭，人种退化，体格羸弱。有人讲我国东南一隅以及南洋的华侨是纯粹的汉人，如果真是如此，那里的人却并不美的。说唐人以胖为美，实则呢，唐人崇尚的是力量。马的时代与我们越来越远了，我们的诗里在赞美着瘦小的毛驴，倦态的老牛，平原上虽然还有着骡，骡仅是马的附庸。

我爱唐美人。

我走进了地下室，一直往里走，从一九九七年走到五百九十三年，敦煌的佛画曾令我神秘莫测，这些宫女，古与今的区别仅在于服饰，但那丰腴圆润的脸盘，那毛根出肉的鬓发，那修长婀娜的体态，使我感受到了真正的人的气息。看着这些女子，我总觉得她们在生动着，是活的，以至

Peeping into the subterranean hall from the entrance, I felt somewhat like a country bumpkin spying on the goings on in the royal palace. "The beauties are banked up like clouds" is one phrase that seems to describe the streets of the present day. Even if the beauties on the streets are banked up like clouds, they lack the graceful delicacy and simplicity of the clouds. It is always reported that "Tang beauties were plump." This arouses some scepticism in the present day: Should the concubine Yang Yuhuan should be counted as a genuine beauty?

"The beauty is one thousand years old!" A friend who had joined me on this visit declared.

The palace ladies in waiting depicted in the mural are all tall in stature, with elongated noses and almond-shaped eyes, big bosoms and broad hips. They wear gowns which sweep across the ground, being the picture of finesse and charm. All the steeds have rangy posteriors, four slender and steely-strong legs. We can tell that people and animals co-existed in harmony. The spirit of the Tang Dynasty was enthusiastic and cosmopolitan, unrestrained and bold. Only in the present has Western Europe come to enjoy a comparable combination of a prosperous economy, an emancipated culture, and the merging of races. We are always surprised by the athleticism of Western European women and call them "mighty foreign mares," never realising that this phenomenon was to be seen in the early Tang Dynasty too. Women and horses were of a piece. Hence, we lament how the power of the nation slid so drastically after the end of the Tang. The more we were invaded, the further we migrated to the south, adopting an increasingly closed mindset. Our race gradually became atrophied and our physiques grew frailer. Some people argue that the purity of the Han ethnicity is preserved only in the residents of Singapore and the remotest southeast corner

看完这一个去看那一个，侧身移步就小心翼翼，害怕走动碰着了她们。她们是矜持的，又是匆忙的，有序地在做她们的工作，或执盘，或掌灯，或挥袖戏鹅，或观鸟捕蝉，对于陌生的我，不媚不凶，脸面平静。这些来自民间的女子，有些深深的愁怨和寂寞，毕竟已是宫中人，不屑于我这乡下男人，而我却视她们是仙人，万般企慕，又自惭形秽了。

《红楼梦》中贾宝玉那个痴呆呆的形状，我是理解他了，也禁不住说句"女儿是水做的，男人是泥做的了"。看呀，看那《九宫女》呀，为首的梳高髻，手挽披巾，相随八位，分执盘、盒、烛台、团扇、高足杯、拂尘、包裹、如意，顾盼呼应，步履轻盈。天呐，那第六位，简直是千古第一美人呀，她头梳螺髻，肩披纱巾，长裙曳地，高足杯托得多好，不高不低，恰与婉转的身姿配合，长目略低，似笑非笑，风韵卓绝，我该轻呼一声"六妹"了！这样纯真高雅的女子，我坚信当年的画师不是凭空虚构的，一定是照生前真人摹绘，她深锁宫中，连唐时也不可见的，但她终于让我看到了，我看到了已经千年的美人。

"美人千年已经老了！"同我去看壁画的友人说。

of China. That may well be so, but the folks over there are unprepossessing and lack charm. Whereas the Tang were said to prize plumpness as a sign of beauty, actually what they cared for most of all was power. The era of those horses is sliding ever more distant from us. In our poems we praise dainty donkeys and beaten down oxen. Mules are to be found on the plains, though these are only the vassals of horses.

How I adore Tang beauties.

I walked into the basement hall and headed directly to its depths. From the year of their creation-593AD-to when I come to view them in 1997, the frescoes in Dunhaung managed to cast a mysterious impression on me. As for these royal ladies in waiting, the contrast between ancient times and today is not just an issue of dress. Their round and mellow faces, their hair sprouting from their skin, and their slim and refined bodies made me sense the breath of real people. Looking at those ladies, I always feel they are vivid and alive, so that after I moved from inspecting one to another I maintained a cautious, sideways shuffle out of fear of colliding with them. They seemed reserved yet were in fact busying themselves in the most orderly of fashions. Some of them were bearing salvers, some grasping lamps, and others flicking their baggy sleeves to amuse geese or watching birds and hunting cicadas. When faced with the unfamiliar – me – they neither flattered nor come across as mean. Their expressions were a picture of calm. Those ladies drawn from the ranks of the civilians may be dogged by loneliness, worries and anxieties. But, after all, they were still members of the royal entourage. They may look down on a rustic like me. On the other hand, I regard them as immortal beings and they fill me with profound admiration. I

高山之上蒼
平凹畫之夜

Moutain Top

then felt myself to be humble and inferior.

I understood the frenzied mentality of Jia Baoyu in *The Dream of the Red Mansions*. I could not help but murmur his very words: "Women are made of water; men are made of mud." Look, look at the head lady in *Nine Palace Ladies in Waiting*. Her hair was bound up high and her hands were holding onto either end of the scarf wrapped around her shoulders. Eight others followed on behind, bearing a salver, a casket, a candlestick, a circular fan, a tall-stemmed goblet, a horsetail duster, a parcel, an "s"-shaped jade charm. They processed in unison on graceful steps. Oh heavens, look at the sixth one. Such a timeless, peerless beauty! Her hair was twisted into a coil and a scarf enfolded her shoulders. Her dress brushed along the floor. The goblet was of a perfect height, being neither too tall nor too squat. The ideal companion for her frame, that pivoted so effortlessly. Her eyes are slightly lowered. Unconsciously she broke into a smile. Her grace and elegance knew no limits. I should have addressed her tenderly as "sixth younger sister"! I firmly believed that such a noble and cultivated beauty was not a figment of the artist's imagination, but sketched with a living, breathing model before him. She must have been locked deep inside the royal palace. Even the Tang people themselves must have seldom clapped eyes on such a damsel. But at last I saw her. I saw a millennium-old beauty.

My friend's words suddenly filled me with sorrow. Nevertheless, my friend felt glad that even beauties had to grow old. I didn't rebuke him. Wherever people are made to consider ageing beauty there are always two sides to this matter – joy and tragedy. This complicated attitude might have been shared by those royal and aristocratic personages. When

友人的话，令我陡然悲伤，但友人对于美人老却感到快意。我没有怨恨友人，对于美人老的态度，从来都是有悲有喜的两种情怀，而这种秉性可能也正是皇戚贵族的复杂心理，他们生前占有她，死后还要带到阴间去，留给后世只是老了的美人。这些皇戚贵族化为泥土，他们是什么狗模人样毫无痕迹，而这些美女人却留在壁画里，她们的灵魂一定还附在画上。灵魂当然已是鬼魂，又在墓穴里埋了上千年，但我怎么不感到一丝恐怖，只是亲切，似乎相识，似乎不久前在某一宾馆或大街上有过匆匆一面？我对友人说：你明白了吗，《聊斋志异》中为什么秀才在静夜里专盼着女鬼从窗而入吗？！

参观完了壁画，我购买了博物馆唐昌东先生摹古壁的画作印刷品，我不愿"六妹"千余年在深宫和深墓，现在又在博物馆，她原本是民间身子，我要带她到我家。我将画页悬挂室中，日日看着，盼她能破壁而出。我说，六妹，我不做皇戚贵族宫锁你，我也没金屋藏匿你，但我给你自在，给你快乐，还可以让你牧羊，我就学王洛宾变成一只小羊，让你拿皮鞭不断轻轻打在我的身上。

they were alive, she was their chattel. When they died, they brought her along as a companion into the underworld. Their legacy for future generations was an aged beauty. All those royals and nobles were reduced to dust. Whether human or canine, not a trace was left of their outlines. And yet, those ladies remained in the murals. Their souls must also have been channelled into the paintings. Of course, their souls are the souls of ghosts. They have been buried in tombs for thousands of years. But, I didn't feel the least tinge of terror. I only felt very close to them as if I knew them. It is as though not so long ago I had ran into these ladies in a hotel or out on the street. I told my friend: "Now do you understand why in *Strange Stories from Liaozhai Studio* the talented young men are always expecting a female spirit to fly in though the window?

After visiting the murals, I bought a printed copy of the facsimiles of these artworks produced by Mr. Tang Changdong. I didn't want "sixth younger sister" to be trapped in the one thousand-year old palace or inside the deep tomb now transferred to the museum. Originally, that girl was drawn from the ranks of the ordinary citizenry. I wish I could have brought her home with me. I hung up the replica inside my room in the hope that she would break out through the walls. I said: "Sixth younger sister, I won't trap you as a member of royalty or the aristocrisy. Nor do I have a gold-lined cell to hide you in. But I could offer you freedom and happieness, and also allow you be a shepherdess. Then I shall take my lead from Wang Luobin and transform myself into a small lamb. In that way, you can gently swish your whip against my body."

不能让狗说人话

西安城里，差不多的人家都养了狗，各种各样的狗，每到清晨或是傍晚，小区里，公园中，马路边，都有遛狗的，人走多快，狗走多快，狗走多快，人走多快。狗是家里成员了，吃得好，睡得好，每天洗澡，有病就医，除了没姓氏，名字也都十分讲究。据说城里人口是八百万了，怎么可能呢？没统计狗呀，肯定到了一千万。

这个社会已经不分阶级了，但却有着许多群系，比如乡党呀，同学呀，战友呀，维系关系，天罗地网的，又新增了上网的炒股的学佛的爬山的，再就是养狗的。有个成语是狐朋狗友，现在还真有狗友了。约定时间吧，狗友们便带着狗在广场聚会，狗们趁机蹦呀叫呀，公狗和母狗交配，然后拉屎，翘起一条后腿撒尿，狗的主人，都是些自称爸妈的，就热烈显摆起他家的狗如何的漂亮，乖呀，能殷勤而且多么地忠诚。

You Cannot Let Dogs Talk like People

Almost every household in Xi'an keeps a dog, so there is no shortage of breeds around. Every morning and every dusk, in the communities, in the parks, or along the street, owners will be out exercising their pets. The dogs may keep pace with the walker and the walker may sometimes have to keep pace with the dog. Dogs have become members of the family. They eat well, sleep well, and shower daily. Whenever they fall ill, they go and see a doctor. Lacking as they do a surname, their given names are nevertheless highly individualistic. It is recorded that there are 8 million residents in the city. How can that be? Nobody has taken a census of canines, so they must number upwards of 10 million.

Society is now classless, yet so many sub-groups have emerged. These include fellow villagers or townsmen, classmates, and army comrades. They cast out and weave a vast social web. Presently, there are supplementary groupings like those who surf online, those who play the stock market, those who pursue Buddhism, those who scale mountains, and those who keep dogs. One proverb states: "Friends

忠诚是人们养狗的最大原因吧。人是多么需要忠诚呀，即便是最不忠诚做人的人，他也不喜欢不忠诚的人和动物。因此，这个城里，流浪的狗并不多见，偶尔见到的只是一些走失的狗，而走失的狗往往就又被人收养了。流浪的多是些寻不着活干的人，再就是猫。猫有媚态，却不忠诚，很多猫猫被赶出家门了。

曾有三个人给我说过这样的事：一个是他们夫妇同岳母生活在一起十多年，在儿子上了中学后，老人去世了。这几年他养了一只狗，有一天突然发现狗的眼神很像岳母的眼神，从此，总觉得狗就是他岳母。另一个人，他说他父亲已经去世七八年了，但他越来越觉得家里的狗像他父亲，尤其那走路的姿式，嘴角一抽一抽的样子。还有一个，他家的狗眼睛细长，凡是家里人说话，或是做什么事情，狗就坐在墙脚，脑袋向前倾着一动不动，而眼睛一眨一眨地盯着，神色好像是什么都看着了，什么都听着了。他就要说：到睡房去，去了把门撞上！狗有些不情愿，声不高不低咕哝着，可能在和他犟嘴，但狗能听懂人话，人却听不懂狗话，狗话只是反复着两个音：汪汪。

You Cannot Let Dogs Talk like People

fool around like foxes and dogs." At this point in time, friendships are in fact forged via dogs. When the appointed time comes around, dog-made friends will assemble together in the square with their pets. The animals will jump around and bark, hounds and bitches will copulate, bowels will be discharged, and cocked legs will unleash the geyser. Every owner declares they are a "pa" or "ma" to their companion and show off with vehemence how handsome, how obedient, how attentive, and how faithful they are. Faithfulness is the number one reason for keeping a dog. How desperately people need faithfulness. Even cheats and philanderers cannot stomach infidelity in another man or beast. In this city, you seldom spot a stray dog. Occasionally you made encounter one or two who have slipped their lead, but those who are lost will always be adopted by others. Itinerant folk who wander the streets are invariably unemployed. And then there are cats. Charming as they are, cats are without loyalty. So many of them find themselves driven out of the house.

Three people have told me a dog-related story. One relates how there was a couple who lived together with the wife's mother for over a decade. After their son went to high school, the old lady passed away. The couple raised a dog instead. One day, they suddenly found that its eyes bore a striking resemblance to the deceased biddy. From then on, they were convinced it was her reincarnation. Another fellow said that his father had died seven or eight years ago. Even so, he increasingly had the sensation that the dog was his pa's spitting image. The gait and

我家的狗叫李富贵
壬午季凹畫于橫天轅

My Dog's Name is Rich Noble Li

the twitching mouth were uncanny. There was, moreover, a man who claimed that his dog had narrow slit-like eyes. When the members of the family were talking or engaged in some activity, the dog would perch at the foot of the wall with its head craning forward and its eyes winking at them. Its expression was all-seeing and all-knowing. Then, the owner would say: "Go to your room and sleep. Bump the door closed after you!" The dog groaned with reluctance in a tone that was neither falsetto nor bass. Maybe it was registering its defiance. Anyhow, it could comprehend human words even though people could not understand it. The pet repeated the same word, only in a different tenor: "Wow! Wow!"

All of a sudden, I pondered: How would it be if a dog could speak the language of humans?

Spurred on by this thought, I broke out in a cold, fearful sweat. Oh heavens, if dogs were to be able to speak our language, what a monstrosity that would be! Every day the news would shake the skies and the world would collapse completely! Just think about it. No matter how sweltering hot it became outside, what would happen within these four walls? So many concealed secrets that belonged to the stately world of humanity would be laid bare for those outside to see. These would include how elderly men disported themselves in an undignified fashion, how youngsters showed no filial piety, how curses flew, how there were violent kickings and punching, hanky-panky in the raw, money laundering, bribery, robbery, smoking dope, fencing stolen items, manufacturing counterfeit goods, tax evasion, others being framed,

我突然想，狗如果能说了人话呢？

刚一有这想法，我就吓出一身冷汗，天呀，狗如果能说人话，那恐怖了，每日都有惊天新闻，这个世界就完全崩溃啦！试想想，外部有再大的日头，四堵墙的家里会发生什么呢？老不尊，少不孝，恶言相向，拳脚施暴，赤身性交，黑钱交易，行贿受贿，预谋抢窃，吸大烟，藏赃物，制造假货，偷税漏税，陷害他人，计算职位，日鬼捣棒槌，堂而皇之的人世间有太多不可告之外界的秘密就全公开了。常说泄露天机，每个人都有他的天机，狗原来是天机最容易泄露者，它就像飞机上的黑匣子，就像掌握核按钮的那些大国的总统，令人害怕了。狗其实不是忠诚，是以忠诚的模样来接近各个人的家庭里窃取人私密的特工呀。好的是，这个社会，之所以还安然无恙，仅仅是狗什么都掌握着，它只是不会说人话。上帝怎么能让狗说人话呢？不会的，会说人话它就不是狗了，也没有人再肯养狗。

是的，不能让狗说人话，永远不能让狗说人话。

scheming after positions, and tricks that could screw up a ghost. People always boast how they have uncovered the mysteries of nature. In actual fact, everybody has their own mystery of nature. It turns out that the dog is the most convenient whistleblower. Just like the black box on a plane or the president of a superpower who has his finger on the nuclear button it wields a terrifying potential. To be honest, dogs are not really faithful. They are simply agents who feign an air of loyalty so as to infiltrate the family and poach its secrets. The upside of this situation is that we still have a harmonious society. Why? Simply because a dog can master everything save for human speech. How could God permit canines to speak our tongue? Impossible. A dog who knows the language of man ceases to be a dog at all. No one would be prepared to have them as pets anymore.

Indeed, dogs should not be allowed to speak our language. Never, period.

动物安详

我喜欢收藏,尤其那些奇石、怪木、陶罐和画框之类,且经发现,想方设法都要弄来。几年间,房子里已经塞满,卧室和书房尽是陶罐画框乐器刀具等易撞易碎之物,而客厅里就都成了大块的石头和大块的木头,巧的是这些大石大木全然动物造型,再加上从新疆弄来的各种兽头角骨,结果成了动物世界。这些动物,来自全国各地,有的曾经是有过生命,有的从来就是石头和木头,它们能集中到一起陪我,我觉得实在是一种缘分,每日奔波忙碌之后,回到家中,看看这个,瞧瞧那个,龙虎狮豹,牛羊猪狗,鱼虫鹰狐,就给了我力量,给了我欢愉,劳累和烦恼随之消失。

但因这些动物木石不同,大小各异,且有的眉目慈善,有的嘴脸狰狞,如何安置它们的位置,却颇费了我一番心思。兽头角骨中,盘羊头是最大的,我先挂在面积最大的西

Animals at Ease

I like collecting objects, especially rare stones, malformed wood, pottery jars and picture frames. Once they have caught my eye, I try to obtain them by any means available. In the space of several years my apartment has come to be jampacked, my bedroom and study are stuffed with fragile items such as vessels, frames, musical instruments and cutlery, and my sitting room is a storehouse for boulders and larger items of carpentry. It just so happens that each of these sizeable curios bears the form of an animal. Together with taxidermy heads and horns collected in Xinjiang, they constitute a kingdom of beasts. These animals have been drawn from every corner of China. Some once enjoyed a sentient existence, whilst others were rock or wood from the outset. Crammed together as my escorts, I feel that this is our fate. When I come home after a busy day, I look here and there: Dragons, tigers, lions, leopards, oxen, sheep, pigs, dogs, fish, insects, eagles and foxes. They all bestow power upon me and fill me with joy, extirpating worry and fatigue.

Since these animals vary in size and material, there are those which appear to have kindly eyes and meek countenances. There are those

墙上，但牦牛头在北墙挂了后，牦牛头虽略小，其势扩张，威风竟大于盘羊头，两者就调了过。龙是不能卧地的，就悬于内门顶上。龟有两只，一只蹲墙角，一只伏沙发扶手上。

柏木根的巨虎最占地方，侧立于西北角。海百合化石靠在门后，一米长的角虫石直立茶机前。木羊石狗在沙发后，两个石狮守在门口。这么安排了，又觉得不妥，似乎虎应在东墙下，石鱼又应在北边沙发靠背顶上，龙不该盘于门内顶而该在厅中最显眼部位，羊与狗又得分开，那只木狐则要卧于沙发前，卧马如果在厨房门口，仰起的头正好与对面墙上的真马头相呼应。这么过几天调整一次，还是看着不舒服，而且来客，又各是各的说法，倒弄得我不知如何是好。

一夜做梦，在门口的两个狮子竟吵起来，一个说先来后到我该站在前边，一个说凭你的出身还有资格说这话？两个就咬起来，四只红眼，两嘴茸毛。梦醒我就去客厅，两个狮子依然在门口处卧着，冰冰冷冷的两块石头。

心想，这就怪了，莫非石头凿了狮子真就有狮子的灵

which are ferocious in their faces and mouths. I have wracked my brain over how to arrange them. Among the animal heads and horns, the argali mountain sheep's head is the largest. First of all, I hung it on the western wall, which happened to be the biggest empty space in my home. Once the yak's head assumed its place on the northern wall, in spite of being a smaller specimen it exuded a charisma that overpowered its counterpart. Hence, I swapped them around. A dragon cannot crawl along the ground, so I hung mine on the hallway ceiling. I had two turtles – one that crouched at the corner of the wall and the other that sprawled out on the sofa arm.

The huge tiger fashioned from a cypress root occupied the greatest space. It stood sideways along the northwestern corner of the room. The fossilised sea lily leant against the back of the door. The one-metre-long black antlered rock balanced upright in front of the tea table. A wooden sheep and a stone dog nestled behind the sofa. Two stone lions guard the door. When these were all so organised, I again sensed some problems. It seemed that the tiger belonged at the foot of the eastern wall, the stone fish should be on the back of the sofa to the north. The dragon had no business being on the ceiling outside, but ought to occupy the prime position in the sitting room. The sheep and dog should be separated. That wooden fox deserved to recline in front of the sofa. If the crouching horse were to be positioned by the kitchen door, its upturned head would have to face the real mare's head on the opposite wall. After several days, I implemented these adjustments, though was still not

Sending Fresh Sea Produce over for the Crane

satisfied with the result. Furthermore, everyone who dropped in on me had their own opinions about how to alter the set-up. I was left well and truly bewildered.

One night I dreamt that the two lions at the front door were quarrelling. One growled: "I came here first, so it should be me who has pride of place." The other replied: "You don't half put on airs. And to think of where you came from." The pair then set about biting each other. Four red eyes and two mouthfuls of fur. When I woke up, I entered the sitting room and found the two big cats still crouching by the door – just two icy cold lumps of rock.

I thought this was peculiar. Was it that a stone carved into the likeness of a lion really does have the soul of a lion? The one in front I purchased the year before last from a village in the Southern Mountains. At that time it was in a pigsty. When I stumbled upon it, the farmer said it was just a chunk of rock and if I liked I could just carry it away. On loading it with great difficulty into the car, the chap saw how delighted I was and asked me to revise my offer. After a few rounds of bargaining, I parted company with 25 yuan. This lion was not mighty in appearance, but handsome. It stood upright and gazed ahead into the sky, its demeanour being that of a proud gentleman. The other one was sent by a friend. He owned a stone hitching post and this lion and invited me to choose one of them. I brought back the lion. I appreciated its barbaric appearance. Just like the characters Li Kui and Cheng Yaojin it was not good-looking, but they would continue their onslaught even

魂？前边的那只是我前年在南山一个村庄买来的，当时它就在猪圈里，当时发现了，那家农民说，一块石头，你要喜欢了你就搬去吧。待我从猪圈里好不容易搬上了汽车，那农民见我兴奋劲，就反悔了，一定要付款，结果几经讨价还价，付了他二十五元。这狮子不大威风，但模样极俊，立脚高望，仰面朝天，是个高傲的角色，像个君子。另一只是一个朋友送的，当时他有一个拴马桩和这只狮子，让我选一个，我就带回了这狮子，我喜欢的是它的蛮劲，模样并不好看，如李逵、程咬金一样，是被打破了头仍扑着去进攻的那种。我拍了拍它们，说：吵什么呀，都是看门的有什么吵的？！但我还是把它们分开了，差别悬殊的是互不计较的，争斗的只是两相差不多的同伙，于是一个守了大门，一个守了卧室门。

第二日，我重新调整了这些动物的位置，龙、虎、牛、马当然还是各占四面墙上墙下，这些位置似乎就是它们的，而西墙下放了羊、鹿、石鱼和角虫石，东墙下是水晶猫、水晶狗。龟和狐，南墙下安放了石麒麟，北墙的沙发靠背顶上一溜儿是海百合化石、三叶虫化石、象牙化石、鸵鸟、马头石、猴头石。安置毕了，将一尊巨大的木雕佛祖奉在厅中的

if their heads were smashed open. I patted them and said: "What is there to argue about? You are just the doorkeepers." Finally, I set them apart. Creatures which are chalk and cheese don't vex each other. Those Which are most alike are bound to become rivals. One of the lions went over to protect the main door. The other was moved to watch the bedroom door. The next day I rearranged the position of these animals, so it went: dragon, tiger, and then ox.

The horses, of course, had one of the four walls apiece. Some were hung up and others were on the ground. These spots seemed to belong naturally to them. At the foot of the western wall, I stood sheep, stone deer, fish and the antlered stone. The foot of the eastern wall had crystal cats and dogs, a turtle and a fox as well. The stone *qilin* occupied the foot of the southern wall and on the back of the sofa, which runs along the northern wall there was a row of fossilised sea lilies, trilobites, fossilised ivory, ostrich fossils, stone horse's heads and monkey heads. After all was settled, I set out a huge wooden Buddha statuette on the stone table at the centre of the sitting room and lit a stick of incense for the Buddha. I thought: The power of the Buddha is infinite. He can control both human beings and the animal world alike. On second thoughts, humans are an intelligent species, while animals are only half-intelligent. If the intelligent can have their own spirits, then there must be the spirit of ghosts too. I painted a picture of Zheng Kui and hung it on the back of the front door. Still not believing this was not enough, I copied out some sayings from an ancient Chinese book and pasted these on the wall

一个石桌上,给佛上了一炷香,想佛法无边,它可以管住人性也可以管住兽性的。又想,人为灵,兽为半灵,既有灵气,必有鬼气,遂画了一个钟馗挂在门后。还觉得不够,书写了古书中的一段话贴在沙发后的空墙上,这段话是:碗大一片赤县神州,众生塞满,原是假合,若复件件认真,争竞何已。

至今,再未做过它们争吵之梦,平日没事在家,看看这个瞧瞧那个,都觉顺眼,也甚和谐,这恐怕是佛的作用,也恐怕是钟馗和那段古句的作用吧。

behind the sofa. The bare outline of the paragraph went like this: "A holy land may be only the size of a bowl, but filled with all the living beings from across the world. It may turn out that they are all fakes. If all of them were real, they would compete and argue all the time." To date, I have never again dreamt of them arguing. When I am free at home, I peer at this one and that. I find that they are all pleasing to the eye and co-exist in harmony. This maybe is the effect of the Buddha? Or perhaps this is down to Zheng Kui and the paragraph I transcribed?

荒野地

这原本是庄稼地,却生长了一片荒草。荒草一人余高,繁荣得蓬勃健美。月夜下没有风,亦不到潮露水的时分,草的枝叶及成熟的穗实萧萧而立,但一种声息在响,似乎是草籽在裂壳坠落,似乎是昆虫在咬噬,静伫良久,跳动的是体内的心一颗。扮演着的是《聊斋》里的人物,时间更进入亘古的洪荒,遥遥地听见了神对命运的招引。

月亮在天上明亮着一轮,看得清其中的一抹黑影,真疑心是荒野地的投影,而地上三尺之外便一片迷。夜是保密的,于是产生迟到的爱情。躲过那远远的如炮楼一般的守护庄稼的庵架,一只饥渴的手握住了一只饥渴的手,一瞬间十指被胶合,同时感受到了热,却冷得索索而抖。

一溜黑地蹚过,松软如过草滩,又分明是脚上穿了宽松

The Wild Land

Originally, this terrain was given over to crops, but was then reclaimed by wild grass, which reached the height of a man, being vigorous, fecund and poised. On a moonlit evening no wind blew and it was not yet time for the dew to settle. The blades of grass and its ripened ears stood there quietly. Anyhow, the sound of breathing was palpable as if the seeds themselves were scratching through the husks in an effort to fall down or as though insects were nibbling away at something. Pausing there insilence for a long time, what was actually thumping was the heart inside the onlooker's torso. Like the characters in *Strange Tales from the Liaozhai Studio* the clock seemed to shift back to the ancient primeval wilderness. The gods were to be heard from afar dictating fate.

The moon was clear and bright in the sky, yet shadows were to be made out on its surface. Could these be the reflections of the wild land? On the ground, everything beyond three feet away was shrouded and chaotic. The night was capable of keeping secrets so liaisons were initiated belatedly. Evading the sentry tower-like hut

精神之花是我们生命灿烂

The Flower of Spirit Made Our Life Colourful

which was used for keeping an eye on the crops, a single hungry and thirsty hand grasped hold of another hungry and thirsty hand. Ten fingers were locked together in an instant. At the same time, they both felt the heat, though shivered with cold.

A plot of black earth stretched across the eyeline. The soil was even tenderer than the meadow. Stepping on it felt like one was wearing a pair of ill-fitting oversized shoes. The pitiful farmers had sown a row of potatoes, but the grasses around them prevented them from thriving. On the harvested land the tubers had not even managed to reach the size of a man's fist. The following morning, only two lines of intersecting footprints remained in the fertile soil.

Coming to the centre of the wild meadow, folks could easily lose their bearings. The environment and atmosphere were deep and still. Both body and soul alike urged the interlopers to be seated. Two rocks happened to be planted there. How many years and months had passed for these expectant stones? Even they had grown frigid in their waiting. Wild grasses streamed between the heavens and the earth. The man was also a blade of wild grass, which had another stalk to his side. It was the eyes which did the talking. They conversed about Tang poems and Song *ci*. The moon above their heads was plump. A breeze was expected and did come. The grass bisected the moon into strips and it shimmered and shook. The anonymous insects groaned, spraying out their special odour. After experiencing the *petit mort* several times and being regenerated

的鞋。可怜的农人种下了这一溜洋芋，四周的荒草却使它们未能健长，挖掘过的地上没有收获到拳大的洋芋。肥沃的土地上明日的清晨却能看到两行交织的脚印。

已经是草地的中央了，失却的则是东南西北的方向。境界幽幽。心身在启示着坐下来，恰好有两块石头，等待这石头是多少个年月，石头也差不多等待得发凉了。天地之间，塞涌的是这荒草，人也是荒草的一棵，再有一棵。说话的是眼睛，说尽着唐诗宋词的篇章。头顶上的月亮丰丰满满。需要有点风，风果然而至。草把月划成了有条纹的物件，且在晃动不已。不知名的昆虫在呻吟着，散发着那特有的气味。待到死过去几次，又活过来几次，一切安静了，望月亮又如深下去的一眼井水，来分辨那里面的身影了。

佛殿一样的地方，得到的是心身的和谐，方明白那一溜松软的黑地是通往未来的甬道，铺着毡毯。

生长庄稼的土地却长满了这么多荒草，这是失职的农人的过错吗？但荒草同样在结饱满的果籽，这便是土地的功

several times, everything became peaceful once again. It was awkward to detect shadows under the moonlight, like the peering into the waters of a deep well.

In a precinct as sacred as the Buddha's shrine, body and soul were fused in harmony. They understood that this plot of black earth was the portal to the future, which was overlaid with carpet.

The cropland was fully covered by so many wild grasses. Were undutiful farmers to blame? Needless to say, the wild grass also produced fully-engorged seeds. This was the function of the land. Perhaps people would curse the undutiful farmers. Still, the fragile crops were not as strong as wild grasses. The wild grass thrived without ploughing, fertiliser and proper seasons!

Human beings were restored to their original form because of this grass. How grand and boundless was the night beneath the moonlight.

The hardship and grief in life had produced countless regrets and determities. Whoever overcomes these can acquire good humour, no longer pinning their hopes on dreams and the next life. They may just sit among the wild land like two pieces of rock. They may sit there for hundreds or thousands of years or they may just tarry there for a short while. Anyhow, that would be enough.

Leaving the wild land, another place is sparse with grass. It is a land for growing melons, maybe pumpkins and watermelons. Surely, they do not harvest what they have been expecting. The melon patch

能。失职的农人或许要诅咒的,而娇弱无能的庄稼没有荒草这么并不需要节令、耕作、肥料而顽强健壮啊!

因为草、人归复了原本的形态,这个月下夜晚是这么苍茫壮阔。

生之苦难与悲愤,造就着无尽的残缺与遗憾,超越了便是幽默的角色,再不寄希望于梦境和来世,就这么在荒野地中坐下,坐下如两块石头。或许坐上百年上千年,或许很短的一别,但已够了。

走出了荒野地,另一处草浅的地方,仍发现了曾是长过瓜果的,是南瓜或是西瓜,肯定的也是未收获到要收获的东西,瓜田早废了,瓜叶腐败为泥,而绳一样纵横的瓜蔓却还发白的将也已为泥的印缀在地上。踏着这白绳的空格走,像是游戏。突然就会想起月亮上的那一株桂树,还有那一位勇敢的却砍不断树身的吴刚。

而毕竟有这么一块荒野地。

has long lain fallow. The leaves of the melon vines have turned to fetid mud, yet the vines, though withered and white, still crisscross like ropes, leaving their imprints on the ground. Walking along the grid formed by these white ropes is akin to playing a game. One can suddenly bring to mind the laurel on the moon and the brave Wu Gang who could not hack through its trunk.

After all, such a wild land did exist.

情

Emotion

两代人

一

爸爸,你说你年轻的时候,狂热地寻找着爱情。可是,爸爸,你知道吗?就在你对着月光,绕着桃花树一遍一遍转着圈子,就在你跑进满是野花的田野里一次一次打着滚儿,你浑身沸腾着一股热流,那就是我;我也正在寻找着你呢!爸爸,你说你和我妈妈结婚了,你是世上最幸福的人。可是,爸爸,你知道吗?就在你新喜之夜和妈妈合吃了闹房人吊的一颗枣儿,就在你蜜月的第一个黎明,窗台上的长明烛结了灯彩儿,那枣肉里的核儿,就是我,那光焰中的芯儿,就是我。——你从此就有了抗争的对头了。

Two Generations

I

Pa, you said that when you were young, you sought after love madly. But, Pa do you know? When you were circling around the peach tree in full blossom under the moonlight, when you were somersaulting in the fields full of wild flowers, a kind of boiling stream was rushing around your body. That was me, and I was looking for you too. Pa, you said that when you got married to my mother, you were the happiest man in the world. But Pa, do you know? When you were sharing in the date that those teasing friends dangled over you on your wedding night; and on the first daybreak of your honeymoon, as the everlasting candle on the windowsill burnt down into a knot - the core of the date was me, I was the wick of the lamp. From then on, you began to have a rival.

二

爸爸，你总是夸耀，说你是妈妈的保护人，而善良的妈妈把青春无私地送给了你。可是，爸爸，你知道吗？妈妈是怀了谁，才变得那么羞羞怯怯，似莲花不胜凉风的温柔；才变得绰绰雍雍，似中秋的明月丰丰盈盈？又是生了谁，才又渐渐褪去了脸上的一层粉粉的红晕，消失了一种迷迷丽丽的灵光水气？爸爸，你总是自负，说你是妈妈的占有者，而贤惠的妈妈一个心眼儿关怀你。可是，爸爸，你知道吗？当妈妈怀着我的时候，你敢轻轻撞我一下吗？妈妈偷偷地一个人发笑，是对着你吗？你能叫妈妈说清你第一次出牙，是先出上牙，还是先出下牙吗？你的人生第一声哭，她听见过吗？

三

爸爸，你总是对着镜子忧愁你的头发。你明白是谁偷了你的头发里的黑吗？你总是摸着自己的脸面焦虑你的皮肉。你明白是谁偷了你脸上的红吗？爸爸，那是我，是我。在妈

II

Pa, you've always boasted that you are my mother's guardian. My kind mother offered her youth unselfishly to you. But Pa, do you know? After the conception, who was it that made my mother become shy and made her as tender as a waterlily unable to bear the chafe of the cold wind, and who was it that caused her to grow plump and full-figured like the Mid-autumn moon? After giving birth, who was responsible for her pink face losing its glamour and that charming feminine sheen? Pa, you've always been so self-conceited and claimed you were my mother's occupier, yet it was my virtuous mother who lavished her concern upon you. But, Pa do you know? When I was in my mother's womb, dare you pound me gently? When my mother smiles alone secretly is it for you? Can my mother tell you when it was you started to teethe? Which of your teeth appeared first – was it an upper or a lower one? Did she hear the first wail of your life?

III

Pa, you're always worrying about your white hairs before the mirror. Do you know who stole the darkness from them? You often stroke your face and worry about your complexion. Do you know who spirited away its red? Pa, it was me, me. In front of my mother,

妈面前，咱们一直是决斗者，我是输过，你是赢过，但是，最后你是彻底地输了的。所以，你嫉妒过我，从小就对我不耐心，常常打我。爸爸，当你身子越来越弯，像一棵曲了的柳树，你明白是谁在你的腰上装了一张弓吗？当你的痰越来越多，每每咳起来一扯一送，你明白是谁在你的喉咙里装上了风箱吗？爸爸，那是我，是我。在妈妈的面前，咱们一直是决斗者，我是输过，你是赢过，但是，最后你是彻底地输了。所以，你讨好过我，曾把我架在你的脖子上，叫我宝宝。

四

啊，爸爸，我深深地知道，没有你，就没有我，而有了我，我却是将来埋葬你的人。但是，爸爸，你不要悲伤，你不要忌恨，你要深深地理解：孩子是当母亲的一生最得意的财产，我是属于我的妈妈的，你不是也有过属于你的妈妈的过去吗？啊，爸爸，我深深地知道，有了我，我就要在将来埋葬了你。但是，爸爸，你不要悲伤，你不要忌恨，你要深深地相信，你曾经埋葬过你的爸爸，你没有忘记你是他的儿子，我怎么会从此就将你忘掉了呢？

we have been rivals. I lost and you won, but in the end you lost outright. So you envied me and were impatient towards me, often beating from when I was young. Pa, when your figure became more and more stooped, like a bowing willow tree, do you know who put a kink in your waist? When your phelgm increases in volume and you wheeze incessantly, do you know who installed those bellows in your throat? Pa, it was me, me. In front of my mother, we have been rivals. I lost and you won, but in the end you lost outright. So you flattered me, let me scramble around your neck and called me "honey."

IV

Oh, Pa, I fully understand that there would no me without you. But when I appeared, I would become the one who will bury you in the future. Even so, Pa, don't feel sad, don't feel envy and hatred. This you should fully understand: the child is its mother's proudest treasure. I belong to my mother. Didn't you too once belong to yours? Oh, Pa, I fully understand that when I appeared, it was as the one who would bury you in the future. Even so, Pa, don't feel sad, don't feel envy and hatred. You should fully understand: once you buried your own father, you did not forget that you were his son. How ever can I forget you then?

我不是个好儿子

在我四十岁以后，在我几十年里雄心勃勃所从事的事业、爱情遭受了挫折和失意，我才觉悟了做儿子的不是。母亲的伟大不仅生下血肉的儿子，还在于她并不指望儿子的回报，不管儿子离她多远又回来多近，她永远使儿子有亲情，有力量，有根有本。人生的车途上，母亲是加油站。

母亲一生都在乡下，没有文化，不善说会道，飞机只望见过天上的影子。她并不清楚我在远远的城里干什么，唯一晓得的是我能写字，她说我写字的时候眼睛在不停地眨，就操心我的苦，"世上的字能写完？！"一次一次地阻止我。前些年，母亲每次到城里小住，总是为我和孩子缝制过冬的衣物，棉花垫得极厚，总害怕我着冷，结果使我和孩子都穿得像狗熊一样笨拙。她过不惯城里的生活，嫌吃油太多，来人太多，客厅的灯不灭，东西一旧就扔，

I am not a Good Son

Only after reaching the age of forty and meeting frustrations in my decades-long, hard-fought, high-flying career, did I realise my faults as a son. The greatness of a mother lies in that she not only gives birth to her own flesh and blood, but in how she also never expects her son to do anything in return. Whether her son ends up far away or stays within her sight, she is the one who will succour to his sense of kinship and strength, keeping him conscious of his roots and base. On the life's journey of a man, his mother serves as his filling station.

My mother stayed in the countryside all her life and was illiterate, tongue-tied with words. The closest she ever came to aeroplanes was spotting their shadows in the sky. She was not clear about what I occupied myself in the distant city; she only knew that I could write words. She informed me that when I scribbled away my eyes blinked all the time. Then she would become worried about the misery I might be enduring. "Can you never finish writing out all the words in the world?" Again and again she tried to halt me in my tracks. Several years ago, when my mother came to reside in the city for a short while, she would pass her time sewing winter garments and other items for my child and I. Fearing that we might catch a chill, she would always stuff extra cotton wadding into whatever she was making. As a result when we

说:"日子没乡下整端。"最不能忍受我打骂孩子,孩子不哭,她却哭,和我闹一场后就生气回乡下去。母亲每一次都高高兴兴来,每一次都生了气回去。回去了,我并未思念过她,甚至一年一年的夜里不曾梦着过她。母亲对我的好是我不觉得了母亲对我的好,当我得意的时候我忘记了母亲的存在,当我有委屈了就想给母亲诉说,当着她的面哭一回鼻子。

母亲姓周,这是从舅舅那里知道的,但母亲叫什么名字,十二岁那年,一次与同村的孩子骂仗——乡下骂仗以高声大叫对方父母名字为最解气的——她父亲叫鱼,我骂她鱼,鱼,河里的鱼!她骂我:蛾,蛾,小小的蛾!我清楚了母亲是叫周小蛾的。大人物之所以是大人物,是名字被千万人呼喊,母亲的名字我至今没有叫过,似乎也很少听老家村子里的人叫过,但母亲不是大人物却并不失却她的伟大,她的老实、本分、善良、勤劳在家乡有口皆碑。现在有人讥讽我有农民的品性,我并不羞耻,我就是农民的儿子,母亲教育我的忍字,使我忍了该忍的事情,避免了许多祸灾发生,而我的错误在于忍了不该忍的事情,企图以委屈求全却未能求全。

wore her handiwork, the youngster and I would look like loping bears. She was not accustomed to life in the city, complaining that the food was too greasy and we had too many visitors and that the light in the sitting room was always on and that we threw away everything as soon as it became old. She said: "Life here isn't as orderly as it is in the country." The thing she found it hardest to bear was how we beat and scolded our child. The infant did not cry, yet she would. After we had patched matters up, she would become annoyed and go back to the country. Each time, she would arrive here joyfully, but leave in a temper. After she had gone, I did not miss her. Year in year out I did not even dream about her at night. My mother's compassion towards me was never appreciated for what it was. When success turned my head, her very existence slipped my mind. Yet, whenever I nursed a grievance or felt wronged, I wanted to tell her about it and grizzle in front of her.

My mother's surname was Zhou. I learnt that from my maternal uncle, but I didn't know her given name. Once when I was twelve years old I was exchanging curses with another child in the village – in the countryside the best way to vent one's gall is to yell out the names of your adversary's parents. That girl's father's name was Fish, so I blurted out "Fish, fishy Fish lives in the river!" She jeered back: "Moth! Moth! Piffling Moth!" I then knew that my mother was called Little Moth Zhou. A big shot is a big shot simply because his name is chanted by thousands of people. Up until then I had never spoken out my mother's name. I had seldom heard our neighbours in our village use that name. Although she was not a great luminary, her stature was not diminished by this preclusion. Her honesty, simplicity, goodness, and industry were universally acknowledged in my hometown. Nowadays, there are those who deride me for retaining the bearing of a farmer. I don't feel ashamed of that. I am

七年前，父亲做了胃癌手术，我全部的心思都在父亲身上。父亲去世后，我仍是常常梦到父亲，父亲依然还是有病痛的样子，醒来就伤心落泪，要买了阴纸来烧。在纸灰飞扬的时候，突然间我会想起乡下的母亲，又是数日不安，也就必会寄一笔钱到乡下去。寄走了钱，心安理得地又投入到我的工作中了，心中再也没有母亲的影子。老家的村子里，人人都在夸我给母亲寄钱，可我心里明白，给母亲寄钱并不是我心中多么有母亲，完全是为了我的心理平衡。而母亲收到寄去的钱总舍不得花，听妹妹说，她把钱没处放，一卷一卷塞在床下的破棉鞋里，几乎让老鼠做了窝去。我埋怨过母亲，母亲说："我要那么多钱干啥？零着攒下了将来整着给你。你们都精精神神了，我喝凉水都高兴的，我现在又不至于喝着凉水！"去年回去，她真的把积攒的钱要给我，我气恼了，要她逢集赶会了去买个零嘴吃，她果然一次买回了许多红糖，装在一个瓷罐儿里，但凡谁家的孩子去她那儿了，就三个指头一捏，往孩子嘴一塞，再一抹。孩子们为糖而来，得糖而去，母亲笑着骂着"喂不熟的狗"，末了就呆呆地发半天愣。

母亲在晚年是寂寞的，我们兄妹就商议了，主张她给

the son of a farmer. My mother told me to have tolerance. I have tolerated everything that I should and, consequently, have sidestepped many calamities. My fault lies in that I have shown forbearance to those who did not deserve it, and have tried unsuccessfully to make concessions in order to secure my aim.

Seven years ago, my father had an operation for stomach cancer. My whole heart and concern were focused upon him. When he passed away, I still dreamt constantly about him. He continued to have a sickly pallor. When I woke up, I would feel sorrowful and weep, then buy some touch paper to burn for him. Once the ashes from the paper had flown away, my thoughts would immediately switch to my mother in the countryside. I would become restless for days. I would then send some money to her. After it had been dispatched, I could once more burrow myself into work with my mind at rest and a clear conscience. Her shadow never loomed in my heart. In my village, everyone praised me for sending her money. However, I came to understand that doing this did not mean I cherished her deep down. Rather I was trying to rectify my own psychological imbalance. My mother could not bring herself to spend this gift. I heard my younger sister say that she had found no place to store it, so rolled the notes up and stuffed them into the cotton shoes under the bed. The rats very nearly pilfered them as bedding. I complained about this to my mother, though she her response was: "What's the use of me having so much cash? I will just save up my spare change and pay you back in full when I can manage it. As long as you are all happy and in good health I'm content to make do with cold water! But right now I'm not in so pathetic a state that I have to drink un-boiled water!" Last year when I went back, she did indeed reimburse the money she had saved. I was antagonised and asked her to go to the country fair and buy some nibbles. She did so and brought

大妹看管孩子，有孩子占心，累是累些，日月总是好打发的吧。小外甥就成了她的尾巴，走到哪儿带到哪儿。一次婆孙到城里来，见我书屋里挂有父亲的遗像，她眼睛就潮了，说："人一死就有了日子了，不觉是四个年头了！"我忙劝她，越劝她越流下泪来。外甥偏过来对着照片要爷爷，我以为母亲更要伤心的，母亲却说："爷爷埋在土里了。"孩子说："土里埋下什么都长哩，爷爷埋在土里怎么不再长个爷爷？"母亲竟没有恼，倒破涕而笑了。母亲疼孩子爱孩子，当着众人面要骂孩子没出息，这般地大了夜夜还要噙着她的奶头睡觉，孩子就羞了脸，过来捂她的嘴不让说。两人绞在一起倒在地上，母亲笑得直喘气。我和妹妹批评过母亲太娇惯孩子，她就说："我不懂教育嘛，你们怎么现在都英英武武的？！"我们拗不过她，就盼外甥永远长这么大。可外甥如庄稼苗一样，见风生长，不觉今年要上学了，母亲显得很失落，她依然住在妹妹家，急得心火把嘴角都烧烂了。我想，如果母亲能信佛，每日去寺院烧香，回家念经就好了，但母亲没有那个信仰。后来总算让邻居的老太太们拉着天天去练气功，我们做儿女的心才稍有了些踏实。

back a great quantity of brown sugar which she tipped into a porcelain jar. Whenever kids came to her place, she would dig three fingers in there and plug a pinch of sugar into their mouths. The children came for the sweet stuff and went away sated. My mother would smile and scold: "Greedy puppies – you're all take, take, take and no give!" Afterwards, she would stare blankly for a long while.

My mother's later years were lonely. We siblings discussed the issue and decided that she could care for my younger sister's children. Tiring as it might prove the time would pass more easily when she had the youngsters on her heart. My little nephew duly became her tail, following her wherever she went. Once, the grandma and grandson came to the city. Her eyes grew moist when she saw the portrait of my deceased father hanging in the study. She said: "When a man is dead, it's easy to count the number of his days. I didn't realise that four years have passed." I promptly tried to change the subject. Still, the more I tried to, the more tears dribbled from her eyes. My little nephew came forward impetuously and asked for "Grandpa" in front of the photo. I thought this would make her more brokenhearted, but she explained: "Your Grandpa was buried under the earth." The child replied: "Anything that's buried grows up again. How come my Grandpa hasn't grown out?" To my surprise, mother was not irritated; instead she broke into a smile. My mother doted on the child and in public she would upbraid him for being without shame. He seemed to be growing physically bigger, but every night would still go to sleep with her nipple in his mouth. The child would then be flushed with shame and come over to gag her lips with his hand. The grandmother and grandson would wrestle on the ground and, being out of breath, she would smile out of breath. My younger sister and I criticised her for pampering him. She conceded: "I've never known an education myself, but all of

小时候，我对母亲的印象是她只管家里人的吃和穿，白日除了去生产队出工，夜里总是洗萝卜呀，切红薯片呀，或者纺线，纳鞋底，在门闩上拉了麻丝合绳子。母亲不会做大菜，一年一次的蒸碗大菜，父亲是亲自操作的，但母亲的面条擀得最好，满村出名。家里一来客，父亲说：吃面吧。厨房一阵案响，一阵风箱声，母亲很快就用箕盘端上几碗热腾腾的面条来。客人吃的时候，我们做孩子的就被打发着去村巷里玩，玩不了多久，我们就偷偷溜回来，盼着客人吃过了，有剩下的。果然在锅底里就留有那么一碗半碗。在那困难的年月里，纯白面条只是待客，没有客人的时候，中午可以吃一顿苞谷糁面，母亲差不多是先给父亲捞一碗，然后下些浆水和菜，连菜带面再给我们兄妹捞一碗，最后她的碗里就只有苞谷糁和菜了。那时少粮缺柴的，生活苦巴，我们做孩子的并不愁容满面，平日倒快活得要死，最烦恼的是帮母亲推磨子了。常常天一黑母亲就收拾磨子，在麦子里掺上白苞谷或豆子磨一种杂面，偌大的石磨她一个人推不动，就要我和弟弟合推一个磨棍，月明星稀之下，走一圈又一圈，昏头晕脑的发迷怔。磨过一遍了，母亲在那里筛箩，我和弟弟就趴在磨盘上瞌睡。母亲喊我们醒来再推，我和弟弟总是说磨好了，

you are doing well for yourselves." We could not out-manouevre her, so only hoped that the kid would remain just as he was forever. Nonetheless, my nephew, like the crops, thrived once he had the blast of the wind upon him. Before we realised it was time for him to enrol at school this year, my mother seemed quite lost. She continued to live in my younger sister's home. She was so anxious that the pent up fire in her heart would break out and cause her lips to be chapped. I thought that if my mother was a believer in Buddhism, she could go to the temple everyday to burn incense and chant *sutras* on her return home. My mother had no such faith. Later, the old grandmothers around her pulled her outdoor to practice *qigong* breathing exercises. Then we siblings felt a semblance of relief.

In my childhood I had the impression that my mother only took care of the food and clothing in the family. During the daytime she would go out to work with the Production Brigade and in the evening she was always rinsing radishes and slicing sweet potatoes or spinning thread and fashioning shoe soles. Otherwise, she would be weaving hemp, fastening the ends of the fibres onto the door latch. My mother didn't know how to prepare fancy fare. Once a year, my father would be responsible for the single grand steaming bowl, though my mother was a skilled hand at kneading noodles. For this she was renowned all over the village. Whenever a visitor dropped by at our home, my father would say "let's have noodles." Then we would hear the sound of the chopping board and the bellows. After a while, my mother would bring in several bowls of piping hot noodles, using the abacus as a tray. As the guests tucked in the children would be sent out to play in the lanes. Before long, we would sneak back stealthily to spy on how much the guests had eaten and if there were any leftovers. As expected, there was roughly a bowl-and-a-half swilling

母亲说再磨几遍,需要把麦麸磨得如蚊子翅膀一样薄才肯结束。我和弟弟就同母亲吵,扔了磨棍怄气。母亲叹叹气,末了去敲邻家的屋子,哀求人家:二嫂子,二嫂子,你起来帮我推推磨子!人家半天不吱声,她还在求,说:"咱换换工,你家推磨子了,我再帮你……孩子明日要上学,不敢耽搁娃的课的。"瞧着母亲低声下气的样子,我和弟弟就不忍心了,揉揉鼻子又把磨棍拿起来。母亲操持家里的吃穿琐碎事无巨细,而家里的大事,母亲是不管的,一切由当教师的星期天才能回家的父亲做主。在我上大学的那些年,每次寒暑假结束要进城,头一天夜里总是开家庭会,家庭会差不多是父亲主讲,要用功学习呀,真诚待人呀,孔子是怎么讲,古今历史上什么人是如何奋斗的,直要讲两三个小时。母亲就坐在一边,为父亲不住吸着的水烟袋卷纸媒,纸媒卷了好多,便袖了手打盹。父亲最后说:"你妈还有啥说的?"母亲一怔方清醒过来,父亲就生气了:"瞧你,你竟能睡着?!"训几句。母亲只是笑着,说:"你是老师能说,我说啥呀?"大家都笑笑,说天不早了,睡吧,就分头去睡。这当儿母亲却精神了,去关院门,关猪圈,检查柜盖上的各种米面瓦罐是否盖严了,防备老鼠进去,然后就收拾我的行李,然后一个人去

around the bottom of the cauldron. During those years of hardship, pure wheat flour noodles were only ever used to entertain guests. If no visitors were around, we would satisfy ourselves with a lunch of cracked corn porridge mixed with noodles. My mother would invariably ladle out some noodles for my father. She would then season the porridge with pickles and diced vegetables, serving the mixture to each of the children in turn. Last of all, her bowl would only contain only cracked corn and vegetables. In that period food and wood as well were at a premium. Life was stark, but we kids never wore a worried expression. We were as bouyant as it was possible to be. The most vexing thing for us was to help our mother turn the grindstone. Usually she would begin to clean the stone after nightfall. She sifted together white corn and beans as a prelude to processing a composite flour. So huge was the grindstone that she could not rotate it unaided. She would ask my younger brother and I to take hold of the handle at the same time. Sporadic were the stars and bright the moon as we trod circuit after circuit around the axis. We persisted until our heads were dizzy and numb. When the first batch was ground, mother would sieve the grain. My younger brother and I would doze off, resting our heads against the stone. She would then rouse us and want to set us to work again, though we would insist "That's enough, that's enough." Nevertheless, she said that it needed to be ground several more times until the bran was as thin as mosquito wings. We two would quarrel with her and toss aside the handle in pique. My mother would sigh and head for the neighouring homes to ask for assistance, saying "Sister-in-law, could you please get up and help me turn the stone?" For a lot time there was no reply, yet she continued to beg, imploring: "I repay you in kind; help you when you do the same job ... The boys are off to school tomorrow, I daren't risk them missing class." My brother and I couldn't bear to see our

灶房为我包天明起来吃的素饺子。

父亲去世后,我原本立即接她来城里住,她不来,说父亲三年没过,没过三年的亡人会有阳灵常常回来的,她得在家顿顿往灵牌前贡献饭菜。平日太阳暖和的时候,她也去和村里一些老太太们抹花花牌,她们玩的是两分钱一个注儿,每次出门就带两角钱三角钱,她塞在袜筒。她养过几只鸡,清早一开鸡棚,一一要在鸡屁股里揣揣有没有蛋要下,若揣着有蛋,半晌午抹牌就半途赶回来收拾产下的蛋。可她不大吃鸡蛋,只要有人来家坐了,却总热惦着要烧煎水,煎水里就卧荷包蛋。每年院里的梅李熟了,总摘一些留给我,托人往城里带,没人进城,她一直给我留着,"平爱吃酸果子",她这话要唠叨好长时间,梅李就留到彻底腐烂了才肯倒去。她在妹妹家学练了气功,我去看她,未说几句话就叫我到小房去,一定要让我喝一个瓶子里的凉水,不喝不行,问这是怎么啦,她才说是气功师给她的信息水,治百病的,"你要喝的,你一喝肝病或许就好了!"我喝了半杯,她就又取苹果橘子让我吃,说是信息果。

mother laying herself at the mercy of others, so we rubbed our noses and retrieved the handle. She assiduously took care of all the mundane matters in the household, such as cooking and providing clothes. By contrast, if major events arose, the last say was reserved for my father, who was a teacher and returned home only on Sundays. During the years when I was a university student, on the final evening of my summer or winter vacation our family would hold a meeting. The main speaker was invariably my father. He would emphasise how we should study, urge us to treat others with sincerity, stress the sayings of Confucius, and relate stories of how folks had achieved success by graft in both ancient times and the present day. As he held forth for two or three hours, mother would sit at his side rolling tapers for his water-pipe. After she had twisted so many, she was apt to nod off. As last, he would pronounce: "Does mother have her pennyworth?" She would then jolt awake and he would scold her, saying: "You see. How can you fall asleep?" Some further words of blame would ensue. She could only smile and reply: "You are a teacher. You are able to rabbit on. What can I say?" Everybody would laugh, point out that it was too late, and head for bed in their various directions. At this moment, my mother would become high spirited. She would go and latch the courtyard gate and the pigsty, and check all the jars of perishables on the counter to see if the lids were secure against rodents. After everything was done, she would enter the kitchen alone and prepare boiled vegetable dumplings for my breakfast the next morning.

Following my father's passing, I at first intended to bring her to live in the city. She refused and said that my father's third anniversary had not come around yet. She maintained that within this period, the soul of the deceased would often migrate home for a visit. She was duty-bound to offer up food before the altar at every meal

我成不成为什么专家名人，母亲一向是不大理会的，她既不晓得我工作的荣耀，我工作上的烦恼和苦闷也就不给她说。一部《废都》，国之内外怎样风雨不止，我受怎样的赞誉和攻击，母亲未说过一句话。当知道我已孤单一人，又病得入了院，她悲伤得落泪，要到城里来看我，弟妹不让她来，不领她，她气得在家里骂这个骂那个，后来冒着风雪来了，她的眼睛已患了严重的疾病，却哭着说："我娃这是什么命啊？！"

我告诉母亲，我的命并不苦的，什么委屈和劫难我都可以受得，少年时期我上山砍柴，挑百十斤的柴担在山砭道上行走，因为路窄，不到固定的歇息处是不能放下柴担的，肩膀再疼腿再酸也不能放下柴担的，从那时起我就练出了一股韧劲。而现在最苦的是我不能亲自伺候母亲！父亲去世了，作为长子，我是应该为这个家操心，使母亲在晚年活得幸福，但现在既不能照料母亲，反倒让母亲还为儿子牵肠挂肚，我这做的是什么儿子呢？把母亲送出医院，看着她上车要回去了，我还是掏出身上仅有的钱给她，我说，钱是不能代替了孝顺的，但我如今只能这样啊！母亲懂得了我的心，她把钱收了，紧紧地握在手里，再一次整整我的衣领，摸摸

time. In her spare time, when the weather was warm, she would trundle off to the village to play cards with the other old grandmas. The standard stake was only one or two cents, so she carried with her twenty or thirty cents in loose notes stuffed down the back of her sock. Early in the morning she would open the chicken coop and poke a finger up each hen's rear end, testing for eggs. If they were on the brink of laying, she would break off her card game halfway through and come home and collect the bounty. Even so, she herself would seldom ate eggs. When guests were visiting, she would announce that she was going to boil water, but when she came back she was bearing a pot with poached eggs inside. Every year, when plums ripened in the courtyard, she would always ask people to take some for me in the city. Should no one be willing to act as courier, the fruit would be stored until my return. "Ping, he is fond of sour fruit." Those words would hover on her lips for ages. She wouldn't tip the fruits away until they were rotted to mush. She trained herself in the practices of *qigong* at my younger sister's home, so that when I dropped in to see her, she would drag me over to the side room after the briefest of conversations. She urged me to drink cool water from a bottle, telling me that I had no choice. On asking her why, she answered that this was the "information water" from a *qigong* master and could cure the whole gamut of illnesses. She said: "You should drink. Afterwards, your liver ailment may be cleared up completely." I consumed half. She then brought out apples and oranges to eat, introducing these similarly as "information fruits".

My mother never cared if I would become a big-shot or a specialist. Neither did she know the honour of my occupation. I never shared with her the tribulations and gloom encountered in my work. When *The Abandoned Capital* whipped up a storm both at home and abroad, she never passed a single comment on whatever

我的脸,说我的胡子长了,用热毛巾捂捂,好好刮刮,才上了车。眼看着车越走越远,最后看不见了。我回到病房,躺在床上开始打吊针,我的眼泪默默地流下来。

praise or attack was meted out on me. But when she heard that I was ill and in hospital alone, she shed sad tears and wanted to visit me in the city. My brothers and sisters forbade her and were unwilling to be her escorts. She was enraged and poked an accusing finger at each of them in her home. Later, she arrived in the midst of the storm and gale. Something was certainly amiss with her eyes, though still she wept and said: "What kind of a fate has my kid run into?"

I informed my mother that my lot was far from poor. I could put up with every variety of wrong and suffering. In my adolescent years I would carry fifty kilos of firewood on my shoulders and walk along the mountain paths. As the paths were narrow, one could not rest load until a particular resting place had been reached, no matter how painful your shoulder and legs were. From then on I cultivated a kind of power of forebearance. The bitterest issue for me at present was that I was unable to wait on my mother in person. With my father being gone, I as the eldest son should take the responsibility for allowing her to live out her dotages happily. Nonetheless, I was not in a position to care for her now and, on she was consumed with worry about me. What kind of a son was I? Accompanying my mother out of the hospital, as she was about to clamber on the bus to go back, I took out all the money in my pocket and gave it to her, saying: "Money cannot be any substitute for filial piety. But this is all I can do now." She understood me and accepted the wad, gripping it tightly in her palm. Once again, she shook my collar until it was arranged in good order and then touched my face, observing that my beard was too long. A hot towel should be applied as a compress and then the whiskers neatly shorn away. I could see the bus crawling gradually away until I lost sight of it. I returned to my ward, lay on my bed, and reinserted the drip, with tears rolling silently down from my eyes.

Scribbled on my ward, 27th November 1993

写给母亲

人活着的时候，只是事情多，不计较白天和黑夜。人一旦死了日子就堆起来：算一算，再有二十天，我妈就三周年了。

三年里，我一直有个奇怪的想法，就是觉得我妈没有死，而且还觉得我妈自己也不以为她就死了。常说人死如睡，可睡的人是知道要睡去，睡在了床上，却并不知道在什么时候睡着的呀。我妈跟我在西安生活了十四年，大病后医生认定她的各个器官已在衰竭，我才送她回棣花老家维持治疗。每日在老家挂上液体了，她也清楚每一瓶液体完了，儿女们会换上另一瓶液体的，所以便放心地闭了眼躺着。到了第三天的晚上，她闭着的眼是再没有睁开，但她肯定还是认为她在挂液体了，没有意识到从此再不醒来，因为她躺下时还让我妹把给她擦脸的毛巾洗一洗，梳子放在了枕边，系在

Written for My Mother

When people are alive, they are not so mindful about day and night because they can only occupy themselves with a finite number of matters. Once a person has passed away, the days pile up. According to my reckoning, in twenty days' time it will be the third anniversary of my mother's death.

During these three years, I have been seized by a queer sensation, namely I have felt that my mother is not actually gone. I have also felt that my mother shares the sense that she has not departed. It is said that dying is like going to sleep, but while the sleeper knows he must slumber on a bed he does not know when exactly he will drift off. For fourteen years, my mother lived together with me in Xi'an. After a serious illness, the doctor confirmed that all of her organs were in a state of terminal exhaustion. I then decided to send her back to our home village of Dihua, where she might continue to receive medical care. Every day, in my village, she knew that once one bag of intravenous medicine was spent, her children would feed another into the drip. She simply closed her eyes and lay

Mother

down there at ease. On the third night, her closed eyes did not open, but she was certain that the drip remained attached. She clearly did not anticipate that thereafter she would never regain consciousness because when she lay down she asked my younger sister to wash her facecloth. The comb lay beside her pillow. The key tied to her belt stayed fastened. She did not convey her final wishes.

Three years ago, whenever I sneezed I would always ask "who is missing me?" My mother loved to crack jokes. She would pick up where I left off and say "who is missing? Your mother is missing you!" During these three years, I have sneezed with greater regularity. Usually, when I am late for a meal or stay up for too long I shall sneeze. When I sneeze I think of my mother and I am certain that my mother is still missing me.

My mother is missing me. She does not believe that she has passed away. I am even more convinced that she is still alive. This feeling is especially intense when I stay quietly alone at home. Often, when I am writing I will suddenly hear that my mother is calling me. The voice is real and sincere. On hearing her call, I will customarily twist my head to the right. Before, my mother used to perch on the edge of the bed in the room to the right-hand side. When I craned over and began to write, she would stop walking around and not make a peep. Instead she would keep her eyes fixed on me. After having stared at me for a long time, she would call out for me and then ask, "Can you ever finish writing out all the words

裤带上的钥匙没有解,也没有交代任何后事啊。

三年以前我每打喷嚏,总要说一句:这是谁想我呀?我妈爱说笑,就接茬说:谁想哩,妈想哩!这三年里,我的喷嚏尤其多,往往错过吃饭时间,熬夜太久,就要打喷嚏,喷嚏一打,便想到我妈了,认定是我妈还在牵挂我哩。

我妈在牵挂着我,她并不以为她已经死了,我更是觉得我妈还在,尤其我一个人静静地待在家里,这种感觉就十分强烈。我常在写作时,突然能听到我妈在叫我,叫得很真切,一听到叫声我便习惯地朝右边扭过头去。从前我妈坐在右边那个房间的床头上,我一伏案写作,她就不再走动,也不出声,却要一眼一眼看着我,看得时间久了,她要叫我一声,然后说:世上的字你能写完吗?出去转转么。现在,每听到我妈叫我,我就放下笔走进那个房间,心想我妈从棣花来西安了?当然是房间里什么也没有,却要立上半天,自言自语我妈是来了又出门去街上给我买我爱吃的青辣子和萝卜了。或许,她在逗我,故意藏到挂在墙上的她那张照片里,我便给照片前的香炉里上香,要说上一句:我不累。

Written for My Mother

in the world? Go out and walk for a while." Now, whenever, I think hear my mother calling me I will lay down my pen and walk into the room. I wonder if my mother has come to Xi'an from Dihua? Of course, there is nobody in the room, but I will stand there for a long time and say to myself that my mother has returned, but popped out onto the street to buy my favourite green peppers and radishes. Or perhaps, she is pulling my leg by deliberately hiding behind her portrait hung on the wall? I will then burn incense in the censing bowl in front of the picture and add one sentence: "I am not tired."

Over those three years, I have composed dozens of articles for others, but never written one single character for my mother. This is because in the eyes of their children all mothers are great and kind. I do not want to repeat this cliché. My mother was an ordinary woman with bound feet. She was illiterate and her household registration certificate was still that of a peasant. However, my mother was so important to me. After a long, long time the thought of her illness no longer brings my heart into my mouth. And yet whenever I prepare to venture to a distant place there is no longer anybody to nag me to do this and that. When I am given fine food and drink, I no longer know to whom I should send them.

In my home in Xi'an, I have not moved a stick of furniture in the room where my mother formerly lived. Everything has been left in its original state. However, I have never glimpsed my mother's shadow. Again and again, I have repeated gravely to myself: "My

整整三年了,我给别人写过十多篇文章,却始终没给我妈写过一个字,因为所有的母亲,儿女们都认为是伟大又善良,我不愿意重复这些词语。我妈是一位普通的妇女,缠过脚,没有文化,户籍还在乡下,但我妈对于我是那样地重要。已经很长时间了,虽然再不为她的病而提心吊胆了,可我出远门,再没有人啰啰唆唆地叮咛着这样叮咛着那样,我有了好吃的好喝的,也不知道该送给谁去。

在西安的家里,我妈住过的那个房间,我没有动一件家具,一切摆设还原模原样,而我再没有看见过我妈的身影。我一次又一次难受着又给自己说,我妈没有死,她是住回乡下老家了。今年的夏天太湿太热,每晚被湿热醒来,恍惚里还想着该给我妈的房间换个新空调了。待清醒过来,又宽慰着我妈在乡下的新住处里,应该是清凉的吧。

三周年的日子一天天临近,乡下的风俗是要办一场仪式的,我准备着香烛花果,回一趟棣花。但一回棣花,就要去坟上,现实告诉着我,妈是死了,我在地上,她在地下,阴阳两隔,母子再也难以相见,顿时热泪肆流,长声哭泣啊。

mother is not dead. She has gone to live in the countryside." This summer it is too hot and humid. Every night when the heat and humidity wakes me, in a trance I think that I should install a new air-conditioner for my mother. When I spring back to my senses, I comfort myself that my mother is living in a new place in the countryside. That place must be cool.

The date of the third anniversary is drawing near. As per to the custom of the countryside we should hold a special ceremony. I am preparing candles, incense, and fruit, ready to go back to Dihua. But once I return to Dihua, I have to visit her grave. The reality is that my mother has passed away. I am on the ground and she is beneath it. Life and death separate us. The mother and son can never cross paths again. Tears cascade down my face accompanied by a long wail.

在女儿婚礼上的讲话

我二十七岁有了女儿,多少个艰辛和忙乱的日子里,总盼望着孩子长大,她就是长不大,但突然间她长大了,有了漂亮,有了健康,有了知识,今天又做了幸福的新娘!我的前半生,写下了百十余部作品,而让我最温暖的也最牵肠挂肚和最有压力的作品就是贾浅。她诞生于爱,成长于爱中,是我的淘气,是我的贴心小棉袄,也是我的朋友。我没有男孩,一直把她当男孩看,贾氏家族也一直把她当作希望之花。我是从困苦境域里一步步走过来的,我发誓不让我的孩子像我过去那样的贫穷和坎坷,但要在"长安居大不易",我要求她自强不息,又必须善良、宽容。二十多年里,我或许对她粗暴呵斥,或许对她无为而治,贾浅无疑是做到了这一点。当年我的父亲为我而欣慰过,今天,贾浅也让我有了做父亲的欣慰。因此,我祝福我的孩子,也感谢我的孩子。

Speech on my Daughter's Wedding

My daughter was born when I was twenty-seven years old. How many hard and busy days have I lived through expecting her to grow up. It seems that she was reluctant to do so. And then it happened in the blink of an eye. She now has elegance, health and knowledge. Today, she has become a happy bride. In the first half of my life, I wrote more than one hundred literary works. But the most heartwarming and fretful task, which was the biggest source of pressure, was my Jia Qian. She was a child of love and grew up enfolded in love. She is my merry, mischievous imp and my consoling cotton coat, not to mention my friend as well. I have never had a son of my own, so always treated her as a boy. The whole Jia clan too regarded her as a flower in bud. I myself was compelled to walk one step at a time through adverse conditions and tribulations, so swore that my child would never know the life of want I had known. Realising that "It is not easy to live in Chang'an," I encouraged her to strive and strive to become stronger. It was imperative that she should show compassion and tolerance. During more than two decades, I may have variously scolded her harshly or employed a strategy

女大当嫁，这几年里，随着孩子的年龄增长，我和她的母亲对孩子越发感情复杂，一方面是她将要离开我们，一方面是迎接她的又是怎样的一个未来？我们祈祷着她能受到爱神的光顾，觅寻到她的意中人，获得她应该有的幸福。终于，在今天，她寻到了，也是我们把她交给了一个优秀的俊朗的贾少龙！我们两家大人都是从乡下来到城里，虽然一个原籍在陕北，一个原籍在陕南，偏偏都姓贾，这就是神的旨意，是天定的良缘。两个孩子生活在富裕的年代，但他们没有染上浮华习气，成长于社会变型时期，他们依然纯真清明，他们是阳光的、进步的青年，他们的结合，以后的日子会快乐、灿烂！在这庄严而热烈的婚礼上，作为父母，我们向两个孩子说三句话。第一句，是一副对联："一等人忠臣孝子，两件事读书耕田。"做对国家有用的人，做对家庭有责任的人。好读书能受用一生，认真工作就一辈子有饭吃。第二句话，仍是一句老话："浴不必江海，要之去垢；马不必骐骥，要之善走。"做普通人，干正经事，可以爱小零钱，但必须有大胸怀。第三句话，还是老话："心系一处。" 在往后的岁月里，要创造、培养、磨合、建设、维护、完善你们自己的婚姻。今天，我万分感激着爱神的来临，它在天空星界，江河大地，也在这大厅里，我祈求着它

of "cultivation by noninterference." There can be no doubt that Jia Qian has achieved all I required of her. Once in the past, my father felt pleased and delighted in me. Today, Jia Qian herself has made me pleased and delighted as a father. So I offer to her – my child – my blessings and thanks.

It is natural for a girl to marry when she becomes an adult. In recent years, as she has grown in age, her mother and I have felt our feelings towards her become more and more complex. On the one hand, she was bound to leave us. On the other, what kind of future would await her? We prayed that she might enjoy Cupid's blessings and find her ideal soulmate so she could own the happiness that was rightfully hers. At last, she has discovered these things. Today we will hand her over to Jia Shaolong, an excellent and handsome young fellow. Our two families both moved to the city from the countryside. The homeland of one was in Northern Shaanxi and the other Southern Shaanxi, yet coincidentally they both shared the surname Jia. This is the will of Cupid and the destiny of the heavens. These two young people inhabit a rich and prosperous era. They have remained uncorrupted by the trend towards vanity and vulgar display. They have lived through the epoch of social transformation, yet have kept pure and clear. This couple is bright and forward-thinking. Their married life promises to be contented and full of colour! On this solemn and heartening wedding day, I should like to convey three sentences on behalf of their parents. First of all, a couplet:

First-class folk, faithful ministers, filial offspring, have
Two tasks to fulfill: reading books and ploughing fields.

永远地关照着两个孩子！我也万分感激着从四面八方赶来参加婚礼的各行各业的亲戚朋友，在十几年、几十年的岁月中，你们曾经关注、支持、帮助过我的写作、身体和生活，你们是我最尊重和铭记的人，我也希望你们在以后的岁月里关照、爱护、提携两个孩子，我拜托大家，向大家鞠躬！

Try to be a worthy servant to one's nation and a dutiful relative at home. Reading renders life full. Conscientious labour keeps food on the table. My second sentence is another old chestnut:

As long as you can rinse the grease off your body, there's no need to bathe in the river or ocean.

As long as the horse is good at trotting, it needn't set its eyes on the steeplechase.

Be an ordinary citizen and work in earnest. You may very well catch the pennies, but broadmindedness is necessary as well. The third sentence is yet another cliché:

Your hearts should be bound together.

In days to come, you must seek for innovation, cultivate yourself, grow accustomed to each other's pace and plan, protect and perfect your marriage. Today, I feel grateful for the descent of Cupid. He rests on every star in the cosmos, in the rivers, the seas and on the land. He is also here in this great hall. I pray that these two children will know his blessings forever. What's more, I am thankful to all our relatives and friends from every walk of life who have come from all points of the compass to attend this event. In the past decade and those before it, you have shown your concern, support, and help to my writing and to my health and my life. You are the people I respect the most. Your names are carved into my heart. I sincerely hope that in future days, you will give your concern, love, care and guidance to them. I beseech you all and bow before every one of you!

思

Meditation

说话

我出门不大说话,是因为我不会说普通话,人一稠,只有安静着听, 能笑的也笑,能恼的也恼,或者不动声色。口舌的功能失去了重要的一面, 吸烟就特别多,更好吃辣子,吃醋。

我曾经努力学过普通话,最早是我补过一次金牙的时候,再是我恋爱的时候,再是我有些名声,常常被人邀请。但我一学说,舌头就发硬,像大街上走模特儿的一字步,有醋溜过的味儿。自己都恶心自己的声调,也便羞于出口让别人听,所以终没有学成。后来想,毛主席都不说普通话,我也不说了。而我的家乡话外人听不懂,常要一边说一边用笔写些字眼,说话的思维便要隔断,越发说话没了激情,也没了情趣,于是就干脆不说了。

On Talking

I seldom talk when I am outside because I have never mastered Standard Chinese. When I find myself in among the crowd, I only listen in silence. I laugh when it is necessary and am annoyed when it is appropriate. Alternatively, I remain calm and collected. My mouth and tongue having relinquished their main functions, I chain smoke and guzzle spicy peppers and vinegar.

More than once I have tried hard to learn to speak Standard Chinese. The first time was when I had my gold fillings inlaid. Then later on, having fallen in love, I made another attempt. On garnering a measure of fame, and with it many invitations, I set myself to the task once more. Alas, whenever it started to gel, my tongue would jam fast in my mouth. Just like a model trying to catwalk on the street, it was a slightly incongruous spectacle. Even I found the sound of my own voice jarring, so was afraid to speak out and let others listen. Ultimately thwarted, I let it drop. Later still, it dawned on me that even Chairman Mao could not speak Standard Chinese, so nor should I. The dialect of my hometown is far harder to understand. It is always the case that

向魚問水

Asking the Fish about Water

On Talking

during conversations I end up writing out what I am trying to say in long hand. My trains of thought and speech are then derailed. The passion for both is lost, so I simply fall silent.

Many years ago, a friend who could speak Standard Chinese accompanied me to Beijing. He was my voicebox. My only regret was that he had a stammer. Despite slowing down to a halting pace, his speech impediment was still obvious. This always gave people the impression that he was short of breath and might be about to pass out at any moment. It so happened that one day someone stopped him on Chang'an and asked for directions. By coincidence, he had a stutter too, so my companion remained silent. Afterwards, I asked him why he hadn't spoken. He replied that "He had a stammer as well. If I did respond to him, he may have thought that I was imitating him and mocking him." He just kept his mouth firmly closed. With that pearl of wisdom from my friend, I was even less willing to speak in the future.

One summer's day, a writer named Mo Yan (the two characters of his Chinese name literally mean "don't speak") was heading to Xinjiang. He sent me a telegram, instructing me to meet him at the railway station in Xi'an. At that time, I had not yet seem him in person before, so I wrote out his name on a board and held it up as I walked about the station. For the whole morning, I remained totally silent. Many people stared at me and didn't say anything either. That day, owing to unforeseen circumstances, Mo Yan could not make it to Xi'an. As the afternoon was drawing near, I was compelled to ask one chap whether

数年前同一个朋友上京，他会普通话，一切应酬由他说，遗憾的是他口吃，话虽说得很慢，仍结结巴巴，常让人有没气儿，要过去了的危险感觉。偏偏一日在长安街上有人问路，这人竟也是口吃，我的朋友就一语未发，过后我问怎么不说，他说，人家也是口吃，我要回答了，那人以为我是在模仿戏弄，所以他是封了口的。受朋友的启示，以后我更不愿说话。

有一个夏天，北京的作家叫莫言的去新疆，突然给我发了电报，让我去西安火车站接他，那时我还未见过莫言，就在一个纸牌上写了"莫言"二字在车站转来转去等他，一个上午我没有说一句话，好多人直瞅着我也不说话，那日莫言因故未能到西安，直到快下午了，我迫不得已问一个人××次列车到站了没有，那人先把我手中的纸牌翻个过儿，说："现在我可以对你说话了。我不知道。"我才猛然醒悟到纸牌上写着"莫言"二字。这两个字真好，可惜让别人用了笔名。我现在常提一个提包，是一家聋哑学校送我的，我每每把"聋哑学校"字样亮出来，出门在外觉得很自在。

不会说普通话，有口难言，我就不去见领导，见女人，

the Number XX train had arrived yet. The fellow first of all turned the board in my hands around and then said: "Now that I am able to speak to you, I must say that I don't know." Only then did the meaning of those two words on my board – DON'T SPEAK – sink in. How wonderful they were and what a pity they had been adopted by another author as his pen-name. These days, when I travel outside I always carry with me a hold-all that was given to me by the "Deaf-Mute School." Whenever I leave the label on the bag exposed, I feel at ease in public.

Since I cannot speak Standard Chinese I am reluctant to meet officials, women and strangers. Gradually, my social activities have all but evaporated and I have been rendered almost inured and mute. Even so, I can curse people. Cursing folk in the dialect of my hometown is cathartic, though actually when I express this I feel crestfallen. I chide myself for being inarticulate and so then try to rally myself. In many of my articles when I describe the place of my birth I never use the phrase "poverty-stricken mountain region." Instead, I write "My birthplace is similar to Mao's birthplace — Shaoshan." When I admit I cannot speak Mandarin, I say: "Standard Chinese is for ordinary people, I am extraordinary!"

A monk once taught me the secret of achieving great things: "Focus your heart on one matter and close your mouth like a bottle." My daughter wrote these characters in her bedroom as her motto. One character was altered, so it read "Focus your heart on one matter and close your mouth like a *ping* (bottle)." Ping is my pet-name. My

见生人，慢慢乏于社交，越发瓜呆。但我会骂人，用家乡的土话骂，很觉畅美。我这么说的时候，其实心里很悲哀，恨自己太不行，自己就又给自己鼓劲，所以在许多文章中，我写我的出生地绝不写"是贫困的山地"，而写"出生的地方如同韶山"，写不会说普通话时偏写道：普通话是普通人说的话嘛！

一个和尚曾给我传授过成就大事的秘诀：心系一处，守口如瓶。我的女儿在她的卧房里也写了这八个字的座右铭，但她写成："心系一处，守口如平。"平是我的乳名，她说她也要守口如爸爸。

不会说普通话，我失去了许多好事，也避了诸多是非。世上有流言和留言，——流言凭嘴，留言靠笔。——我不会去流言，而滚滚流言对我而来时，我只能沉默。

daughter was claiming that she would keep her mouth as tightly closed as her father.

I cannot speak Standard Chinese and have missed out on so many boons, yet have avoided so much strife too. The world is awash with gossips and insinuating notes. Gossip is the product of the mouth and notes the product of the pen. I've never found myself able to share in gossip. However, when gossip comes my way I always keep silent.

辞宴书

老兄：

今晚粤菜馆的饭局我就不去了。

在座的有那么多领导和大款，我虽也是局级，但文联主席是穷官、闲官，别人不装在眼里，我也不把我瞧得上，哪里敢称作同僚？他们知道我而没见过我，我没有见过人家也不知道人家具体职务。

若去了，他们西装革履我一身休闲，他们坐小车我骑自行车，他们提手机我背个挎包。于我觉得寒酸，于人家又觉得我不合群，这饭就吃得不自在了。

On refusing an invitation to a banquet

My older brother:

I shan't be attending the Cantonese style banquet tonight.

There may be so many senior leaders and nouveau riche there this evening. Although I'm also a bureau head, the Chairman of the Federation of Literature and Arts Circles has little chance to peddle his place for profit; he isn't even kept overly occupied. Others never have me in their line of vision and I too look down upon myself. How can I sit in their company? True enough, they know who I am but have never met me before. I've never made their acquaintance and cannot even be sure of their specific ranks.

If I were to go, all of them would be wearing Western-style dinner jackets, whereas I would dress casually. They would be chauffeured over there, whereas I would choose to cycle. They would brandish cellular phones, while I would have nothing but my hold-all. I would feel humble in and of myself, yet they might sense I was being unsociably aloof. All of us would be ill-at-ease as we dined.

If you want to eat, just stick with your friends. The food will

要吃饭和熟人吃得香,爱吃的多吃,不爱吃的少吃,可以打嗝儿,可以放屁,可以说趣话骂娘,和生人能这样吗?和领导能这样吗?知道的能原谅我是懒散惯了,不知道的还以为我对人家不恭,为吃一顿饭惹出许多事情来,这就犯不着了。

酒席上谁是上座,谁是次座,那是不能乱了秩序的,且常常上座的领导到得最迟,菜端上来得他到来方能开席。我是半年未吃海鲜之类,见那龙虾海蟹就急不可耐,若不自觉筷先伸了过去如何是好?即便开席,你知道我向来吃速快,吃相难看,只顾闷头吃下去。若顺我意,让满座难堪,也丢了文人的斯文;若强制自己,为吃一顿饭强制自己,这又是为什么来着?

席间敬酒,先敬谁,顺序不能乱,谁也不得漏,我又怎么记得住?而且又要说敬酒词,我生来口讷,说得得体我不会,说得不得体又落个傲慢。敬领导要起立,一人敬全席起立,我腿有疾,几十次起来坐下又起来,我难以支持。

taste delicious then. You can gorge on more of what you like and spurn what you are not keen on. You can belch, fart, curse, and jape while eating. Can you do these things among strangers? Can you do these things among senior leaders? Familiar folk are inclined to be forgiving because they know that this is my way. Those who are not may very well conclude that I am being disrespectful. It is not worth going to a meal when so much trouble could ensue.

There are, moreover, strict, inviolable rules about who should be seated at the head of the table and who should sit immediately to his side. The senior leader who is given priority has the prerogative to turn up late. The table may have been laid, but the others cannot touch the dishes before he arrives. I've now gone half a year without eating seafood. When I spy lobsters and crabs I cannot restrain myself. What would happen if I couldn't wait and unconsciously stretched out my chopsticks first? You know, even after a banquet has begun I cannot help but bolt my food, my table manners are unsightly, and my mind is fixated on eating. If I were to act on impulse, that would make the others feel awkward and rob me of the gentility of a man of letters. If I had to try and practice self-control, what would be the point of sharing a meal and then not be one's self?

During the rounds of toasts, who should be the first to be saluted? That order too is sacrosanct. You cannot skip inadvertently over any single party. How could I be expected to commit all of this to memory? Furthermore, formal words must embellish a toast. I was not born

我又不善笑,你知道,从来照相都不笑的。在席上当然要笑,那笑就易于皮笑肉不笑,就要冷落席上的气氛。

更为难的是我自患病后已戒了酒。若领导让我喝,我不喝拂他的兴,喝了又得伤我身子。即使是你事先在我杯中盛白水,一旦发现,那就全没了意思。

官场的事我不懂,写文章又常惹领导不满,席间人家若指导起文学上的事,我该不该掏了笔来记录?该不该和他辩论?说是不是,说不是也不是。我这般年纪了,在外随便惯了,在家也充大惯了,让我一副奴相去逢迎,百般殷勤做媚态,一时半会儿难以学会。

而你设一局饭,花销几千,忙活数日,图的是皆大欢喜,若让我去尴尬了人家,这饭局就白设了,我怎么对得住朋友?而让我难堪,这你于心不忍,所以,还是放我过去,免了吧。

几时我来做东,回报你的心意,咱坐小饭馆,一壶酒,

gregarious. I don't know how to express myself correctly. If I were to express myself improperly, people would assume me to be proud and distant. When we offer toasts to senior leaders we are required to stand up. All of those present must get to their feet. I have something wrong with my leg. Rising and sitting down dozens of times that would prove truly unbearable!

What is more, I am not good at smiling. I don't even smile when I'm having my photograph taken. At the banquet I would be compelled to beam broadly, of course, but that expression would be a movement of the skin not felt deep down in the flesh. In this case, an air of discord would hang over the proceedings.

To make matters harder still, I quit drinking because of an ailment. If the senior leaders were to propose a toast, my refusal would deflate their hospitable spirits. Should I knock the stuff back, that would imperil my health. One might simply fill my liquor cup with plain water, but once the ruse had been unmasked everything would be rendered meaningless.

I am ignorant when it comes to officialdom. My articles always put officials on edge. During the banquet if the senior leaders were to deliver advice on writing, ought I to take out a notebook and jot down everything they said? Ought I to argue with them or not? It wouldn't be proper for me to say either "yes" or "no." I have reached that age when I've become accustomed to feeling comfortable outside and I've grown used to being the head of my own household. I'd struggle to act like a slave at

两个人，三碗饭，四盘菜，五六十分钟吃一顿！

　　如果领导知道了要请我而我未去，你就说我突然病了，病得很重。这虽然对我不吉利，但我宁愿重病，也免得我去坏了你的饭局而让我长久心中愧疚啊。

the drop of a hat, affecting humble actions and flattering words.

You have prepared for this banquet, swallowing up thousands of yuan and many days. The purpose is to make everybody happy. If I were to go and be the object of embarrassment, all of that would have been in vain. How could I not regret what I had done? That would be a source of acute discomfort. You couldn't bear to see this happen. So, let me decline and please forgive me.

Sometime in the future I shall return your goodwill by treating you. We can sit in a small inn, order one pot of liquor - just us two chaps, with three bowls of rice and four dishes. You may tuck in heartily for fifty minutes or an hour!

If the senior leaders find out that you did invite me but I declined to go, you can tell them that I've come down with a sudden, serious illness. Although that would be an inauspicious lie, I'd rather be seriously ill than attend the event and spoil it. The pity would well up from the bottom of my heart and last inordinately.

朋友

朋友是磁石吸来的铁片儿、钉子、螺丝帽和小别针,只要愿意,从俗世上的任何尘土里都能吸来。现在,街上的小青年有江湖义气,喜欢把朋友的关系叫"铁哥们",第一次听到这么说,以为是铁焊了那种牢不可破,但一想,磁石吸的就是关于铁的东西呀。这些东西,有的用力甩甩就掉了,有的怎么也甩不掉,可你没了磁性它们就全没有喽!昨天夜里,端了盆热水在凉台上洗脚,天上一个月亮,盆水里也有一个月亮,突然想到这就是朋友么。

我在乡下的时候,有过许多朋友,至今二十年过去,来往的还有一二,八九皆已记不起姓名,却时常怀念一位已经死去的朋友。我个子低,打篮球时他肯传球给我,我们就成了朋友,数年间身影不离。后来分手,是为着从树上摘下一堆桑椹,说好一人吃一半的,我去洗手时他吃了他的一

On Friends

A friend is just like a piece of iron, a nail, a screw, and a safety pin. As long as you wish, you can be the magnet that will draw them out from the dirt of this world. Nowadays, young friends on the streets share a code of brotherhood. They delight in calling their pals "iron brothers". When I first heard this form of address, I thought it meant that their friendship was unbreakable like welded iron. On second thoughts, "iron" is the element attracted by a magnet. When a magnet is jiggled around some of its load may fall away, but other pieces remain attached no matter how violently you shake. If you happened to lose your magnetism then everything will drop away. Last night, I carried over a basin of warm water to wash my feet on the balcony. The moon was hanging in the sky and there was also one in the water in my basin. I suddenly realised that this was how friends should be.

When I was in the countryside, I had a lot of friends. Twenty years have passed by. One or or two of them still keep in touch with me and as for eighty or ninety per cent of the rest I cannot even remember their names. Often I do bring to mind a friend who has now passed away.

半,又吃了我的一半的一半。那时人穷,吃是第一重要的。现在是过城里人的日子,人与人见面再不问"吃过了吗"的话。在名与利的奋斗中,我又有了相当多的朋友,但也在奋斗名与利的过程中,我的朋友交换如四季。……走的走,来的来,你面前总有几张板凳,板凳总没空过。我做过大概的统计,有危难时护佑过我的朋友,有贫困时周济过我的朋友,有帮我处理过鸡零狗碎事的朋友,有利用过我又反过来踹我一脚的朋友,有诬陷过我的朋友,有加盐加醋传播过我不该传播的隐私而给我制造了巨大的麻烦的朋友。成我事的是我的朋友,坏我事的也是我的朋友。有的人认为我没有用了不再前来,有些人我看着恶心了主动与他断交,但难处理的是那些帮我忙越帮越乱的人,是那些对我有过恩却又没完没了地向我讨人情的人。

地球上人类最多,但你一生的交往最多的却不外乎方圆几里或十几里,朋友的圈子其实就是你人生的世界,你的为名为利的奋斗历程就是朋友的好与恶的历史。有人说,我是最能交朋友的,殊不知我的相当多的时间却是被铁朋友占有,常常感觉里我是一条端上饭桌的鱼,你来叨一筷子,他来挖一勺子,我被他们吃剩下一副骨架。当我一个人坐在厕

On Friends

Despite my small stature, he liked to pass the ball to me whenever we played basketball. We became good mates and for years we were like each other's shadow. We parted ways, though, simply because of a bunch of mulberries. We had made a deal that each of us would have half of the fruit. When I went to wash my hands, he ate his half and then mine. At that time people were so poor that eating was the top priority. Now we have become city dwellers, we never greet one another by asking "have you eaten?" In the struggle for fame and affluence, I made lots of friends, but in the process of this struggle my friends proved as ephemeral as the seasons ... some have come along, some have gone away, yet the benches in front of me were always occupied. I totted up a few rough statistics. There have been friends who helped or hurt me when I was in trouble. There have been friends who offered me a hand when I was down on my heels. There have been friends who have helped me to deal with everyday sundry things, and, what is more, certain friends who have chosen to use me and then inflict an unceremonious kick. Some friends have crossed me, and others even caused great trouble by broadcasting my private business, seasoning it with salt and vinegar. It has been my friends who have raised me up and deflated me as well. There are those who have severed ties when they thought me spent and others I have shunned when their behaviour sickened me. In those cases, I took the initiative to break off diplomatic relations with them. By contrast, it is tough to deal with those whose attempts at help actually multiply my troubles, not to mention those who have done something for me but ask me for endless

所的马桶上独自享受清静的时候，我想象坐监狱是美好的，当然是坐单人号子。但有一次我独自化名去住了医院，只和戴了口罩的大夫护士见面，病床的号码就是我的一切，我却再也熬不下一个月，第二十七天里翻院墙回家给所有的朋友打电话。也就有人说啦：你最大的不幸就是不会交友。这我便不同意了，我的朋友中是有相当一些人令我吃尽了苦头，但更多的朋友是让我欣慰和自豪的。

过去的一个故事讲，有人得了病去看医生，正好两个医生一条街住着，他看见一家医生门前鬼特别多，认为这医生必是医术不高，把那么多人医死了，就去门前只有两个鬼的另一位医生家看病，结果病没有治好。旁边人推荐他去鬼多的那家看病，他说那家门口鬼多这家门口鬼少，旁边人说，那家医生看过万人病，死鬼五十个，这家医生在你之前就只看过两个病人呀！我想，我恐怕是门前鬼多的那个医生。根据我的性情、职业、地位和环境，我的朋友可以归两大类：一类是生活关照型。

人家给我办过事，比如买了煤，把煤一块一块搬上楼，家人病了找车去医院，介绍孩子入托。我当然也给人家办过

favours in return.

Human beings are the dominant species across the surface of the world, but those who are to be found within a radius of a few miles form your closest associates. Your circle of friends is in fact the world of your life. Your battle for success can be seen as the process of hating and admiring those you consider your friends. A number of people have observed that I am very capable at making friends, but they never know that the majority of my time has been occupied by my bosom friends alone. Frequently, I've thought of myself as being like a cooked fish lain out on the dining table. Someone poked it with chopsticks and others dug away with a spoon, leaving only a skeleton in the end. When I sit alone on the toilet and enjoy the quiet, I feel how nice it is to be in prison. Of course, I mean in solitary confinement. Once I admitted myself into hospital under an alias. All the doctors and nurses I met were hidden behind surgical masks. I was no longer a name but a number – the digits hanging above my bed. Before the month was out, I could tolerate this no longer and so on the twenty-seventh day I scaled the perimeter wall and called all my friends. Another person commented that my greatest misfortune is my inability to make friends. I cannot entirely agree with this view. A few of my friends brought me all manner of hardships, but the greater part made me feel proud and delighted.

A story from bygone days relates how a man was ill and went to see a doctor. Two doctors lived in the same street. Before the home of one of them, he had the apparition of numerous ghosts. He concluded

Climbing the Ladder

that this fellow must be incompetent and that many patients had died under his care. He then went to the other doctor and saw only a couple of spirits hovering in front of his house. After consulting him, the man's illness was still not cured. A bystander advised him to go back to the first doctor with the herd of ghosts. He explained that this one had treated thousands and thousands of patients, of who only perhaps fifty had expired. The doctor he had been to see had only tried to cure two patients, neither of whom pulled through! It occurred to me that maybe I am just the same as the doctor with many ghosts in front of his home. Judging from the perspective of my career, personality, position and environment, my friends appear to fall into two categories, one of which is those who sincerely care about others.

A few friends offered me everyday assistance. For instance, in buying coal and lending a hand hauling it upstairs. Some chauffeured sick relatives to hospital or found a kindergarten for my child. It goes without saying that I opened doors for them too. I wrote out pieces of calligraphy that they could use to soft-soap officials who ranked above them. I gave them paintings of mine that would smooth the way for them when putting in for a bank loan. I attended birthday dinners for my friends' fathers-in-law. Maybe they helped me a lot; maybe I have helped others more. As long as we have been absolutely sincere and honest to each other, there is no need to keep a tally. We are firm friends all the same.

The other category of friends is those soulmates who find

事,写一幅字让他去巴结他的领导,画一张画让他去银行打通贷款的关节,出席他岳父的寿宴。或许人家帮我的多,或许我帮人家的多,但只要相互诚实,谁吃亏谁占便宜就无所谓,我们就是长朋友,久朋友。

一类是精神交流型。具体事都干不来,只有一张八哥嘴,或是我慕他才,或是他慕我才,在一块谈文道艺,吃茶聊天。在相当长的时间里,我把我的朋友看得非常重要,为此冷落了我的亲戚,甚至我的父母和妻子儿女,可我渐渐发现,一个人活着其实仅仅是一个人的事,生活关照型的朋友可能了解我身上的每一个痣,不一定了解我的心,精神交流型的朋友可能了解我的心,却又常常拂我的意。快乐来了,最快乐的是自己,苦难来了,最苦难的也是自己。

然而我还是交朋友,朋友多多益善,孤独的灵魂在空荡的天空中游弋,但人之所以是人,有灵魂同时有身躯的皮囊,要生活就不能没有朋友,因为出了门,门外的路泥泞,树丛和墙根又有狗吠。

themselves incapable of achieving anything concrete, only being able to cultivate a slick tongue like a parrot. Still, they are happy to share a pot of tea and converse about literature and art because we admire each other's talent. For rather a long time, I took my friends very seriously, ignoring even my relatives, my parents, wife and children. Nevertheless, I gradually found that how one lives one's life is a personal matter. A caring friend may know every mole on my body without understanding my heart. Whereas soulmates who do understand my heart still find themselves doing things contrary to my will. When happiness comes along, you are the one who savours it most deeply, and when suffering arises, you are the one who is worst afflicted.

I do persevere in making friends - the more the merrier. A lonely soul could wander through the empty sky, but people are people simply because they possess both soul and body. Man cannot live without friends. When you leave home, you may have to face adversities – a muddy road outside, thickets and rabid dogs barking at the foot of walls.

Picasso was a Spaniard, a man of genius and lifelong renown. He also could boast friends without number. Many friends seem to have been born to help him, but he had a high turnover of both women and acquaintances. We are unable to emulate his ways. But he did leave a word of wisdom: "A friend is good when he is gone." When I recall those friends who are now estranged or from whom I have cut off contact, my heart chills. But I regain my composure when I recall the good deeds they did for me. My heart had chilled because I took my friends

西班牙有个毕加索，一生才大名大，朋友是很多的，有许多朋友似乎天生就是来扶助他的，但他经常换女人也换朋友。这样的人我们效法不来，而他说过一句话：朋友是走了的好。我对于曾经是我朋友后断交或疏远的那些人，时常想起来寒心，也时常想到他们的好处。如今倒坦然多了，因为当时寒心，是把朋友看成了自己和自己的家人，殊不知朋友毕竟是朋友，朋友是春天的花，冬天就都没有了，朋友不一定是知己，知己不一定是朋友，知己也不一定总是人，他既然吃我，耗我，毁我，那又算得了什么呢？皇帝能养一国之众，我能给几个人好处呢？这么想想，就想到他们的好处了。

今天上午，我又结识了一个新朋友，他向我诉苦说他的老婆工作在城郊外县，家人十多年不能团聚，让我写几幅字，他去贡献给人事部门的掌权人。我立即写了，他留下一罐清茶一条特级烟。待他一走，我就拨电话邀三四位旧的朋友来有福同享。这时候，我的朋友正骑了车子向我这儿赶来，我等待着他们，却小小私心勃动，先自己沏一杯喝起，燃一支吸起，便忽然体会了真朋友是无言的牺牲，如这茶这烟，于是站在门口迎接喧哗到来的朋友而仰天嚯嚯大笑了。

as family members, and did not realise that when all is said and done, a friend is a friend. Friends are spring blossoms, which disappear in winter. A friend may not necessarily be a soulmate. Equally, a soulmate may not necessarily be a friend. A soulmate might not always act as a true man. He may feed off me, consume me, and even malign me. That counts for nothing. An emperor can feed the people of an entire country, so how many people should I offer my help to? Thinking in this way, I miss the benefits of having friends.

This morning, I made another new friend. This fellow complained to me about how his wife was working in a county suburb. For more than a decade, the whole family had not been able to hold a reunion. He asked me to write several pieces of calligrapy for him to offer as gifts to the head of the human resources section. I wrote them for him straightaway. He left me a tin of green tea and a carton of refined cigarettes. When he was gone, I called three or four old friends over to share the happiness. At this moment, they are hastily pedalling their way over here. I will wait for them. Selfishly, I have already brewed and poured a cup of tea for myself and lit a cigarette. All of a sudden, I sense the speechless sacrifice of a true friend. They are just like the tea and cigarette. I shall surely burst into laughter when I greet those noisy and boisterous pals at the door.

敲门

人问我最怕什么？回答：敲门声。在这个城里我搬动了五次家，每次就那么一室一厅或两室一厅的单元，门终日都被敲打如鼓。每个春节，我去郊县的集市上买门神，将秦琼敬德左右贴了，二位英雄能挡得住鬼，却拦不住人的，来人的敲打竟也将秦琼的铠甲敲烂。敲门者一般有规律，先几下文明礼貌，等不开门，节奏就紧起来，越敲越重，似乎不耐烦了，以至于最后咚地用脚一踢。如今的来访者，谦恭是要你满足他的要求，若不得意，就是传圣旨的宦官或是有搜查令的警察了。可怜做我家门的木头的那棵树，前世是小媳妇，还是公堂前的受挞人，罪孽深重。

我曾经是有敲声就开门的，一边从书房跑出来，一边喊：来了来了！来的却都是莫名其妙的角色，几乎干什么的都有，而一律是来为难我的事，我便没完没了地陪他们，

Knocking at the Door

What do people fear the most? The answer is: the sound of knocking at the door. I have moved five times while living in the city. Each time, it was to a single- or two-bedroomed apartment with one sitting room. All day long my door was pounded at like a drum. Every Spring Festival, I would go to the market to buy a pair of "door guardians." These images of the heroes Qin Qun to the right and Jing De to the left, were effective at barring ghostly visitors, but could exercise no power over humans. Folks with their fists even hammered Qin Qun's armour into pieces. Knockers usually follow their own etiquette. The first few taps are polite and civilised. When the door does not open, the pace becomes urgent, heavier and heavier as if they are impatient. At last, they deliver a kick to the door. As for visitors nowadays, those who are modest and polite ask me to offer help with one thing or another. An unwanted guest is about as welcome as a eunuch who is bringing an imperial edict or policemen with a search warrant. How pitiful was the tree whose wood became the door of my home. In its previous life, it must have been a belittled wife or a condemned man flogged in a

我感觉我的头发就这么一根根地白了。以后,没有预约的我坚决不开门,但敲打声使我无法读书和写作,只有等待着他们的走开。贼也是这么敲门的,敲过没有反应就要撬门而入,但我是不怕贼的,贼要偷钱财,我没钱财,贼是不偷时间的,而来偷我时间的人却锲而不舍,连续敲打,我便由极度地反感转为欣赏:看你能敲多久?!门终于是不敲了。可过一会儿,敲声又起,才知敲者并没有走,他的停歇或许是敲累了,或许以为我刚才在睡觉或上厕所,为此敲敲停停,停停敲敲,相信我在家中,非敲开不可。我只有在家不敢作声,越是不敢作声,喉咙越发痒想咳嗽,小便也憋起来,我恨我成了一名逃犯。

狡兔三窟,我想,我还不如只兔子。这么大的城里,广厦千万间,怎么就没有一个别处的秘密房子,让我安静睡一觉和读书写作呢?我当然不敢奢想有深宅大院,有门子在前可以挡驾,有那么一小间放张桌子和小床即可,但我不能。以致于我在任何地方去上厕所,都设想有这么个地方,把蹲坑填了,封了天窗,也蛮好嘛。我的房间从来是一室一厅或二室一厅,前无院子,后无后门,什么人寻我,都是瓮中捉鳖。

courtroom.

I used to open the door as soon as there was a knock. While rushing out from my study I would shout: "Coming, coming." But the waiting visitors were all odd characters from every walk of life. They dropped by seeking help and were troublesome to deal with. Compelled to keep company at all times I could feel my hair whitening, one strand at a time. Latterly, I never opened up for those who had not made an appointment.

The sound of the knocking distracted me from reading and writing. I could only wait for the culprit to leave. Thieves also beat the door in this manner. If there is no answer from the inside they would jemmy their way in. I am not afraid of burglars wanting to swipe loose change or a fortune, for I have neither to hand. Thieves never set out to rob time, but those who do come with that intention prove themselves very persistent. They knock relentlessly. At this point my extreme aversion morphs into admiration. I want to test how long they can keep their hand going. Finally, the knocking ceases. After a while, it resumes and I realise they never actually left. Perhaps they stopped out of exhaustion or maybe they assumed I was asleep or in the bathroom and had a breather before starting again. They must believe I am at home, so are certain to pound the door open. Silence is my only form of resistance. The more I restrain myself, however, the itchier my throat feels and I have the compulsion to cough. My bladder starts to tug, but I cannot risk emptying it. I hate this feeling of being like an escaped convict.

Pottery Jar Loving Writer

A cunning rabbit keeps three warrens. My life is now no better than that of a bunny. In such a sprawling city with thousands upon thousands of rooms and apartments, how come I cannot find a private space to sleep and to read and write in peace? Owning a large and deep courtyard with a doorkeeper is simply a pipe dream. I would gladly make do with a bedsit with a desk. That is not viable. Whenever I squat down in the lavatory, I imagine how pleasant it would be to fill in the pit and seal the skylight, renovating it into my own personal garret. My apartments always have one or two bedrooms and a sitting room without a courtyard in the front or a back door to the rear. I am as easy to root out as a turtle in a jar.

Actually, I am not the kind of man who can cope without friends. When I am not reading and writing, I will ask three or four pals to come and drink, chat about women, and play chess or *mahjong*. But it is always the case that the friends who you pine for do not come, while those you would rather avoid turn up. More than once I have refused to open the door, even leaving my relatives from back home standing out in the cold. They are all busy folks and so leave after a few raps, figuring that I must not be at home. Such was my regret that I stamped my foot and punched my chest. Those I cannot keep away include the following: fans seeking out handwritten calligraphic scrolls to serve as sweeteners to their superiors, folk who are throwing parties of various kinds and think I might add glamour, and idlers who just want to alleviate their boredom. People like that have cartloads of time to squander. If they find

事实是，我并不是个不需要朋友的人，读书写作之余，我也要约三朋四友来喝酒呀，谈天呀，博弈搓麻将。但往往是想念的朋友不来，来的都是不想见的人。我曾坚持不开门，挡住了几次我的从老家来的亲戚，他们是忙人，敲几下以为我不在家就走了，过后令我捶胸顿足。我挡不住的是那些要我写条幅去送他的上级的人，是那些有什么堂会让我去捧场的人，或是他们什么事也没有，顺脚过来要解闷的，他们有的是闲工夫，上午来敲不开门，下午又来敲，今日敲不开明日再来敲，或许就蹲在门外和楼下。他们是猎人，守在那里须等小兽出来。

明代的陈继儒说过：闭户即是深山，闭户哪里又能是深山呢？

或说，那是你红火啊。可我并不红火，红火能住这么小的房子吗？如果我是官人家，客来又有重礼，所求之事谈完即走，走时还得说：不打扰了，您老辛苦，需要休息。找我的双手空空，只吸我的烟，喝我的茶。如果我是歌星影星，从事的就是热闹工作，可我热闹了能写出什么文章？又是读陈继儒的小品，陈先生恐怕在世时也多骚扰，曾想去做隐

you are not in during the morning, they will try again in the afternoon. If today ends in failure, they will seek you out tomorrow. Maybe in the interim they will crouch outside or downstairs with the mien of a hunter, waiting for his small prey.

Chen Jiru in the Ming Dynasty wrote: "A deep mountain appears behind a closed door." How could this be so?

Some may say this is because you are very famous. But I am not a celebrity. How could a person of that ilk occupy such a small apartment? Were I an official, visitors might bring lavish gifts and leave as soon as they had finished talking about the thing with which they wanted to deal. As they are parting, they are bound to say: "I won't disturb you. Sir, you are too busy, and you need a rest." Even so, those who come to me carry with them only two empty hands and polish off my cigarettes and tea. If I were a movie star or a pop singer, my career would be a rowdy affair. How could I compose my works in a rowdy situation? So I went on to read Chen Jiru's prose. Possibly he, like me, found himself interrupted by others for he longed to become a hermit. Anyhow, he once surmised that: "Most hermits till for themselves." I am not strong, so this is the first factor holding me back. I cannot shoot or fish for I abhor killing. That is the second factor holding me back. I am poor for I have no more than two *qing* of land and I do not own eight hundred mulberry trees. This is my third shortcoming. I only drink water and eat plain food and cannot bear hunger and hardships. This is my fourth problem. Just like Mr. Chen, the best I can hope for is to "have a plain

者,但他说:"隐者多躬耕,余筋骨薄,一不能;多钓弋,余禁杀,二不能;多有二顷田,八百桑,余贫瘠,三不能;多酌水带索,余不耐苦饥,四不能。"我同陈继儒一样,我可能者,也是"唯嘿处淡饭著述而已"。但淡饭几十年一贯,著述也只是为了生计和爱好,嘿处竟如此不能啊!想想从事写作以来,过几年就受冲击,时时备受诽谤,命运之门常被敲打,灵魂何时有过安妥?而家居之门也被这般敲打不绝,真是声声惊心。小儿发愿,愿明月长圆,终日如昼,我却盼永远是在夜里,夜里又要落雪下雨,使门永不被敲打。

但这怎么可能呢?我还要活的,我还有豪华的志向,还有上养老下哺小,红尘更深,我的门恐怕还是不停地被人敲打。我的命就是永远被人敲门,我的门就是被人敲的命吧。有一日我要死了,墓碑上是可以这样写的: 这个人终于被敲死了!

meal and write in a quiet place." After dozens of years of surviving on plain meals, for me writing was only a hobby and then a way of making a living. What an insurmountable problem it is to find "a quiet place" and to be able to stay there alone. As I recall, ever since I began to write professionally every few years I have met with criticism or received a thorough tongue-lashing. The door of my fate was always being knocked at. My soul never had the time to rest in tranquillity! The door of my home has been subject to constant knocking as well. The din has truly unsettled my heart. Youngsters always wish to see the round moon all the time and to have perpetual night. As for me, I wish that the night would never end and that there would be snow and rain. Then my door would be left undisturbed.

秃顶

脑袋上的毛如竹鞭乱窜，不是往上长就是往下长，所以秃顶的必然胡须旺。自从新中国的领袖不留胡须后，数十年间再不时兴美髯公，使剃须刀业和牙膏业发达，使香烟业更发达，但秃顶的人越来越多，那些治沙、治荒的专家，可以使荒山野滩有了植被，偏偏无法在自己的秃顶上栽活一根毛。头发和胡子的矛盾，是该长的不长，不该长的疯长，简直如"四人帮"时期的社会主义的苗和资本主义的草。

我在四年前是满头乌发，并不理会发对于人的重要，甚至感到麻烦，朋友常常要手插进我的发里，说摸一摸有没有鸟蛋。但那个夏天，我的头发开始脱落，早晨起来枕头上总要软软地粘着那么几根，还打趣说：昨儿夜里有女人到我枕上来了？！直到后来洗头，水面上一漂一层，我就紧张了，忙着去看医生，忙着抹生发膏。不济事的。愈是紧张地忙着

Bald Head

The hair on people's heads is like bamboo shoots. It spurts forth wildly whether in an upward or downward direction. Hence those who have a bald head are bound to have a vigorous moustache. For decades, ever since the leader of the New China refused to sport a moustache, facial hair fell out of fashion with image-conscious gentlemen. The razor and shaving foam industry no longer prospered. The tobacco industry, however, thrived. More and more bald-headed people began to appear. Experts in land reclamation may be able to turn wild lands and mountains into green plots, but they are powerless to awaken a single follicle on their own bare scalps. The contradiction between head hair and moustaches lies in that the one which should grow does not, yet the one that shouldn't runs riot. It is just like the "socialist seedling" and the "capitalist grass" in the period of the Gang of Four.

Four years ago, my head was thick with black hair. I paid little attention to how much hair mattered in the lives of people and even regarded it as troublesome. My friends would thrust their fingers into my mane and say they wanted to see if there were some bird's eggs in

治，愈是脱落厉害，终于秃顶了。

我的秃顶不同于空前，也不同于绝后，是中间秃，秃到如一块溜冰场了，四周的发就发干发皱，像一圈铁丝网。而同时，胡须又黑又密又硬，一日不剃就面目全非，头成了脸，脸成了头。

一秃顶，脑袋上的风水就变了，别人看我不是先前的我，我也怯了交际活动，把他的，世界日趋沙漠化，沙漠化到我的头上了，我感到非常自卑。从那时起，我开始仇恨狮子，喜欢起了帽子。但夏天戴帽子，欲盖弥彰，别人原来不注意到我的头偏就让人知道了我是秃顶，那些爱戏谑的朋友往往在人稠广众之中或年轻美貌的姑娘面前说："还有几根？能否送我一根，日后好拍卖啊！"脑袋不是屁股，可以有衣服包裹，可以有隐私，我索性丑陋就丑陋吧，出门赤着秃顶。没招无奈变成了率直可爱，而人往往是因为可爱才美丽起来。如此半年过去，我的秃顶又不成新闻，外人司空见惯，似乎觉得我原来就是秃了顶的，是理所当然该秃顶的。我呢，竟然又发现了秃顶还有秃顶的来由，秃顶还有秃顶的好处哩。

there. That summer, though, it began to fall out. When I got up in the morning, I would always find stray strands sticking to the pillow. I would poke fun at myself by musing: "Did a woman lay her head down there last night?" That was until one day, I was washing my hair and found a whole layer of hairs floating on the water. Seized with anxiety, I went to consult the doctor and started to douse my head with growth-stimulating tonic. Nothing had any effect. The more measures I nervously took to remedy the problem, the worse the situation became. Eventually I became a baldy ....

Me becoming a baldy is neither an unprecedented nor isolated phenomenon. Patches of hair remained on the back and temples, but the middle hollowed out like a flat ice rink. The sides where there was still coverage dried out and grew wrinkled like the cables in an iron wire fence. At the same time, my moustache darkened, thickened and became stiffer. If I skipped shaving for only one day, my face would be unrecognisable. The head would be transformed into the face and the face into the head.

Once I became a baldy, the *feng-shui* of my head altered. In other's eyes I was no longer my former self. I assumed a shy air, being reluctant to attend social functions. Damn it! The world is in the grip of desertification. The process has spread to my head. I sank into a humble state. From then on, I started to loathe lions and develop a fondness for hats. Wearing a hat in the summertime, though, was a case of *the more you try to hide, the more you actually expose*. Those who hadn't paid

Meditation

attention to my head before now realised that I was a baldy. Friends who delighted in poking fun at me in crowded places or before pretty ladies would say: "How many do you have left? Can you please give me a single hair? I may auction it off in the future." The head is not your backside. You can't conceal it with clothing and keep it private. I reasoned it just as well to lay bare my ugliness as it was and went out with my forlorn scalp uncovered. In the eyes of others, my helplessness had been transformed into something frank and charming. People always become prettier when they are charming. Half a year has now passed by and my bald head is no longer headline news. Instead it is part of the furniture. Everyone seems to think that if I wasn't a baldy in the first place I should have been one anyway. For me, to my surprise, I found that there are both reasons behind and advantages to having a bald head.

The three main reasons behind having a bald head are:

1. According to folk theory: "Talented men are never top heavy." This theory was drawn from generation after generation of observing visual evidence. So this means that I am smart!

2. Geologists have addressed how: "Grass never grows on mountains with rich mineral deposits." From this standpoint, mine is no ordinary head!

3. Women have long hair, so this is a symbol of femininity. For a long time, mankind has obviously been feminised. A bald head is the counterpoint to this process. God has endowed me with a masculine mission and the heavens invested in me a great duty. If I didn't become

秃顶有秃顶的三大来由:

一、民间有理论:灵人不顶重发。这理论必定是世世代代在大量的实情中总结出来的,那么,我就是聪明的了!

二、地质科学家讲:富矿山上不长草。由此推断,我这颗脑袋已经不是普通的脑袋啦!

三、女人长发,发是雌性的象征。很久以来人类明显地有了雌化,秃顶正是对雌化的反动,该是上帝让肩负着雄的使命而来的。天降大任于我了,我不秃谁秃?!

秃顶有秃顶的十大好处:

一、省却洗理费。

二、没小辫可抓。

三、能知冷知晒。

四、有虱子可以一眼看到。

bald, who else could?

The ten great advantages of being bald are:

1. Saving money on washing and grooming.

2. There are no little pigtails (shortcomings) for others to tug on.

3. Knowing readily when it is hot and cold.

4. Lice are visible at first sight.

5. You are ready to go into battle at any time.

6. Having a tonsure is a sign of mercy.

7. Having no queue to be lopped off as a sign of ostracism.

8. When you get angry there is no hair to stand on end and push off your hat.

9. Enjoying longevity like a turtle.

10. Never having your unwashed hair be mistaken for mould.

Nowadays, I always hum a ditty about being a baldy:

Baldy,

Skin lesion,

Smooth and slippery,

Like a painted gourd,

Without a single hair,

Watermelon, bulb, and silken ball,

Shine all over the world like a moon,

When I sing this song, I think in my heart "What under the heavens is impossible? Hah, as long as there is a moon in the sky I can also give off some light of my own!

五、随时准备上战场。

六、像佛陀一样慈悲为怀。

七、不会被"削发为民"。

八、怒而不发冲冠。

九、长寿如龟。

十、不被误为发霉变坏。

现在,我常哼着的是一曲秃顶歌:秃,肉瘤,光溜溜,葫芦上釉,一根发没有,西瓜灯泡绣球,一轮明月照九州。我这么唱的时候,心里就想,天下事什么不可以干呢。哼,只要天上有月亮,我便能发出我的光来!

三月十五日,我和我的一大批秃顶朋友结队赤头上街,街上美女如云,差不多都惊羡起我们作为男人的成熟、自信,纷纷过来合影,合影是可以的,但秃顶男人的高贵在于这颗头是只许看而不许摸的!

On 15th March, a big group of bald-headed friends and I walked along the streets, our follicly-challenged state on full view. The beauties were banked up like clouds. All of them were surprised and admired the mature, self-confidence of us men folk. They all jammed in to have their picture taken with us. The taking of photographs is not prohibited, though the nobility of a hairless man lies in that his head can only be watched, but never touched!

吃烟

吃烟是只吃不进,属艺术的食品和艺术的行为,应该为少数人享用,如皇宫寝室中的黄色被褥,警察的电棒,失眠者的安定片;现在吃烟的人却太多,所以得禁止。

禁止哮喘病患者吃烟,哮喘本来痰多,吃烟咳咳咔咔的,坏烟的名节。禁止女人吃烟,烟性为火,女性为水,水火生来不相容的。禁止医生吃烟,烟是火之因,医是病之因,同都是因,犯忌讳。禁止兔唇人吃烟,他们噙不住香烟。禁止长胡须的人吃烟,烟囱上从来不长草的。

留下了吃烟的少部分人,他们就与菩萨同在,因为菩萨像前的香炉里终日香烟袅袅,菩萨也是吃烟的。与黄鼠狼子同舞,黄鼠狼子在洞里,烟一熏就出来了。与龟同默,龟吃烟吃得盖壳都焦黄焦黄。还可以与驴同嚎,瞧呀,驴这老烟

On Smoking

Smoking mimics the act of eating only nothing passes into your guts. It is a form of connoisseurship on a par with art appreciation and fine cuisine. Like the bed chambers in the imperial palace, the stun guns used by police officers, and the tranquillisers used by insomniacs, it exists to be used by the few. Nowadays, there are too many smokers and it should be outlawed.

Asthmatics should be forbidden from smoking. They have too much pent-up phlegm. When they smoke they will hack and give cigarettes a bad reputation. Women should be prohibited from smoking since tobacco belongs to the element of fire and the female sex to the element of water. The two cannot co-exist. Physicians should be banned too. Just as smoke is rooted in fire, doctors depend on illness for their livelihood. They are both tied to the cause of certain phenomena, so for them to mix would be taboo. Those with a hare-lip should be proscribed as well, for they cannot balance a cigarette in their mouths. Ditto, gentlemen with lengthy facial hair. Whoever has seen grass growing inside a chimney breast?

鬼将多么大的烟袋锅儿别在腰里!

我是吃烟的,属相上为龙,云要从龙,才吃烟吞吐烟雾要做云的。我吃烟的原则是吃时不把烟分散给他人,宁肯给他人钱,钱宜散不宜聚,烟是自焚身亡的忠义之士,却不能让与的。而且我坚信一方水土养一方人,是中国人就吃中国烟,是本地人就吃本地烟,如我数年里只吃"猴王"。

杭州的一个寺里有副门联,是:"是命也是运也,缓缓而行;为名乎为利乎,坐坐再去。"忙忙人生,坐下来干啥,坐下来吃烟。

A tiny minority would still be permitted to smoke. They would be allowed to live like the Bodhisattva. All day long censers in front of the Buddha statue exhale perfumed clouds, so that he is a fellow smoker. Smokers can jig together with the skunk, which secretes itself in its warren until the stench proves unbearable. Those addicts keep silent together with the turtles. The turtle smokes until its shell is stained sallow. They can also whinny together with the donkeys. Behold, both tuck their pipes about their waists when not in use, but the donkey's is humongous!

I am a smoker. I was born in the Year of the Dragon. Clouds circulate around the dragon. He can only generate these after swallowing smoke. My principle of smoking is that I don't pass out cigarettes to others; I would rather give them money. For it is good to spread out money rather than hoard it. Tobacco is a kind of loyal and faithful retainer who would rather he himself burnt to death. Thus, one should not offer it to others. I firmly believe that man is the product of his environment. Chinese people should smoke Chinese cigarettes. Local people should smoke locally-produced tobacco. For instance, I've stuck to the Shaanxi-made *Monkey King* for years.

A couplet on the architraves of a temple in Hangzhou states:

Whether through fate or luck, persist in your life slowly
Whether for money or for fame, sit here and then leave.

In the midst of a busy life, why should people sit down? Just sit down and smoke.

龙年说龙

中国人有许多崇拜,除了日月山河声光雷电外,也崇拜动物,认为自己的今世都是前世的动物托生,于是年年出生的人就有了鼠牛虎兔龙蛇马羊猴鸡狗猪的属相。这些动物轮流当值,十二年一轮回,每到当值就称本命年。但是,任何当值都是有权在握,主宰一切的,偏偏本命年里该属相者则慌恐,因为一辈人一辈人传下来的经验教训,本命年这一年里顺者一顺再顺,不顺者百事不顺,是一道关口,一个门坎,便得系红腰带,摆酒席,若有好事将一生二,二生三,三生无数,若有不好的事就分为一半,大而化小,小而化了。

我是属龙的,世纪的钟声一过,当年的就是辰龙,而且这一个本命年,四十九岁,百岁之间最厉害的一个,所以,前几日见到几位朋友,都说:今年得给你过生日了!他们说

Talking about the Dragon in the Year of the Dragon

The Chinese people worship so many things. Apart from the sun and the moon, rivers, voice and light, thunder and lightning, they happen to revere animals. They all believe that their present life is the reincarnation of a past existence. Thus, the people born in each year belong to the sign of an animal according to the Chinese Zodiac. The twelve creatures are the rat, the cow, the tiger, the rabbit, the snake, the horse, the sheep, the monkey, the rooster, the dog, and the pig. These animals take their turn to serve on duty. A dozen years forms a complete cycle or *samsara*. The time when a particular creature's duty comes around is known as "the Year of …." Whoever stands on duty has the power to preside over everything. However, those people whose year has arrived may appear cautious and worried. Based on the experiences and lessons handed down from previous generations, if one matter proceeds smoothly for a person in their year all else will follow likewise. If one matter proceeds badly, the contrary will be true. This is a kind of strategic pass, a threshold that has to be negotiated successfully. Those marking their year must wear a red belt and lay out a spread of liquor and dishes for other people. By this means, should one good thing

着，要去商店买上好的红线编成腰带送我，也已商量着要我在什么豪华酒店里请他们客。朋友这么一闹，我蓦地醒悟了：本命年对于当事者并不是有可能出现坎的事，而绝对只是好事，之所以系红腰带，这是在宣告这一年我的命神要当值了，是升堂，是扶上正位，最起码也是像球场上的队长要戴上袖标一样的。以中国的儒家观点，当值也就是做了官，做官威风了得，但做官也就有了社会责任心，不能张狂，不可妄行，是大人还得小心，是圣贤仍要庸行，如此才是公仆，为人民服务，这当然你得鞠躬尽瘁，每事慎其三思了。再者，之所以要设摆宴席，掏着口袋请客，一是众人要捧场起哄，以示祝贺，二是你做官了就得安抚众人，这就是钱宜散不宜聚的道理嘛！

龙在中国人的心目中历来都是至高无上，每个皇帝总以真龙天子自尊，民间里也常是以属龙相得意。那么，新纪元首先轮到辰龙当值，这是多大的吉祥，这是天意哇，国家该要复兴了！北京就修了个中华世纪坛，中央领导人在寒夜里出席典礼，场面盛大，而举国上下到处在张灯结彩，摆龙台，舞龙灯，能怎么表现就怎么表现，据报载，竟在几个省

transpire, it will beget a second, then a third, and so on. Thereafter, should one bad thing eventuate, the ill-fortune will be split in half. The big trouble will shrink to being minute, before disappearing altogether.

I was born in the Year of the Dragon. The hours of the dragon are 7 am-9 am. When the new century chimes in, this year will be my animal's year. I shall be 49 years old – a crucial stage on the route to reaching a century. Several days ago when I gathered with friends they said that they must hold a party for me. As soon as they expressed those sentiments, they headed for the shop to purchase red cord, which could be woven into a belt for me. They further debated how I ought to treat them in a luxury hotel. Their fussing made me suddenly realise that he who enjoys the year of his animal does not necessarily have to suffer ill-fortune, but may have an unremittingly positive experience. Why should I wear a red belt? It is to declare that this year the god of my life will be on duty. It is just like a becoming a trial judge, being promoted to the position of chair, or at least being the captain of a football team who is permitted to wear a red armband on the pitch. From the standpoint of Chinese Confucianism, the person on duty is raised to be an official. Officials are powerful and mighty. Nevertheless, they have social responsibilities of their own. They should be neither flippant, nor arrogant, nor presumptuous. "Great saints behave prosaically, great people act cautiously." Only in this way are those public servants capable of serving the people. Of course, you must spare no efforts in performing one's duty and, what is more, think over what you plan to do at least twice. In addition, you should lay the table and treat others. For, on the one hand, people may come over to cheer and congratulate. On

有书法家在广场巨笔书写百平方米的龙字。看到这种场面，属龙相的人当然喜之不禁，各个年龄层的，龙子龙孙们，都视作普天之下的盛典全是在为我们祝寿哩。

十二个属相中，为什么选中鼠牛虎兔龙蛇马羊猴鸡狗猪，而不是狮子老虎大象，我一直弄不明白。但十一个属相都是具体的动物，唯独龙是虚拟的。中国人崇拜动物，而崇拜到图腾地步的只有龙，龙又是综合众多动物的形象而想象出来的，这就说明中国人其实宗教的意识并不浓重，他们的思维注整体，重象征，缺乏穷极物理。这种思维当然就决定了中国的哲学和艺术的特点，从庄子的逍遥游到老子的大象无形，以及音乐、绘画、医学、武术、棋艺、园林莫不如是，即便是文学作品，也讲究的是生活流程的演义，悠然见南山的意境，不着一字尽得风流的形式美感，它虽不如西方悲剧意识的强烈而使读者为之震撼，但宽博幽远韵味绵长在清明祥和中而使灵魂得以了提升。

东西方的文化差异人人都在口头上说着，在当今全球风靡美国文化的背景下，却更多的人，尤其那些时髦的

the other, as an official you should console others. The way of the world dictates that money is better spread than hoarded.

In the minds of Chinese people, the dragon reigns supreme and almighty. Every emperor declared himself a "True Dragon" and "the Son of Heaven." In accordance with folk customs, ordinary people too feel proud at have been born in the Year of the Dragon. While an American athlete is overjoyed to wear stars and stripes shorts, we Chinese sing a song 'Offspring of the Dragon.' Then in this new era, the animal on duty is the dragon from 7 am – 9 am. What great fortune. This is the will of heaven. The country is going to be rejuvenated! A Chinese Millenium Monument has been built in Beijing. The leaders of the central government attended the opening ceremony in the chilly evening. The spectacle was magnificent. All over China people hung up lamps and colourful ribbons. They set up dragon platforms and hoisted dragon lanterns. Whatever they did, they went to town on it. According to the news reports, in some provinces calligraphers used gigantic brushes to write out the character for "dragon" in their local square. The letters stretched for 100 metres. On witnessing these marvels, those born in the Year of the Dragon are indeed overjoyed. Those children and grandchildren of the dragon, though they vary in age, all look upon these grand ceremonies as if they are their own birthday party.

Why is it that the rat, the cow, the tiger, the rabbit, the snake, the horse, the sheep, the monkey, the rooster, the dog, and the pig were chosen in the compilation of the Chinese Zodiac and not the lion, the bear, and the elephant? For a long time I have been confused about this. Of the group, eleven are real animals. Only the dragon is mythological. Chinese people worship animals,

学者，偏拿西方的东西抵毁中国的东西，拿西方人的奶油比中国人的白菜，殊不知肉食动物虽比草食动物高大强壮，但虼蚤专吸腥血虼蚤仍是小，大象吃草大象却是庞然大物。说到这里，又有一个问题出现了，龙是中国人综合诸多动物而想象出来的，那么，综合性的东西若作为图腾是非常美好的，充满了大气和庄严，可现实的动物界里，是老虎你就长你的老虎，是狮子你就长你的狮子，而既要像这样又要像那样，就只会沦落到蜥蜴、鸡、壁虎、四脚虫那样的丑陋和弱小。任何借鉴都只能是精神的吸取，而不是能达到吃了牛肉就长牛肉的。我们的祖先创造了龙的形象后，不幸的是他们的后代也就有了以龙的形象组合原理而企图生硬拼凑的习性，使我们在多个领域里发生着失误，以致今日常常听到一种哀叹：明明是龙种为什么就生下了跳蚤呢？

龙在中国产生的年代已经够古老的了，但给我们的印象，清代的龙是绣在国旗上的，民间又是铺天盖地的到处是龙。时下之国人，动辄说到民族传统，精神的源头不是溯之而上的，只是目光短浅到王气衰微的明清时代，以致

but they only revere the dragon as a totem. The dragon is a composite of so many creatures and images. This evinces that the religious consciousness of the Chinese is not so strong. They pay much attention to integrity and symbolism in their way of thinking, but lack the spirit of philosophical investigation. This, of course, determined the characteristics of Chinese philosophy and art. From Zhuangzi's "happy excursion" to Laozi's "a great form has no contours" Chinese music, painting, medicine, martial arts, playing chess and gardening all follow this pattern. Even literary works focus on evoking the process of life and try in their artistic conception to view the Southern Mountain in a leisurely glance. In aesthetic form, they strive to obtain elegance and grace without using any words. They may not shock the audience in the same manner as Western tragedies, but they offer catharsis to the reader through evoking a deep and remote flavour and through clarity and harmony.

Everybody talks about the cultural differences between East and West. Nowadays, American culture holds sway all over the world. More and more people, especially scholars who follow the trend of the times, favour parroting Western viewpoints so as to attack the Chinese. They compare Western cream to Chinese cabbage. But they do not know that although flesh-eating animals are larger and stronger than those that graze, a flea may be tiny but it sucks blood. An elephant is huge colussus, yet it eats grass. On reaching this point, another question rears its head. The dragon is an imaginary animal fabricated by the Chinese based on components of numerous entities. If we regard a synthetic being as a totem, this would be great. It would be abounding with solemnity and grandeur. In the real world of animals, if you are a tiger you must grow like a tiger, if you are a lion you must grow like a lion. Should you grow in both that way and this, you will degenerate into something small and grotesque like

今日庆典龙年，凡舞龙耍狮者，凡敲锣击鼓者，所穿服装不是汉唐之衣，亦不是中山装西服，皆色彩式样恶俗不堪的明清时打扮，只差一点要再拖个油乎乎的脏辫子了。还可以看看，现在充斥我们生活中的龙的形象是多么小气和萎缩！

原本龙是虚拟之物，但越来画龙的、做龙的人全把龙弄得越具体化，似乎天底下果真有了个龙的活物，如他们炕头上的猫和门后头卧着的狗。我是欣赏古人对龙的刻画，它综合着鱼、虎、马、蛇、鹿和猪的诸多形象，但它绝对不是鱼、虎、马、蛇、鹿和猪的，西周战国时期出土的玉器上、铜鼎上、兵器上的龙的形象是最简练而充满了张力，它往往在具体的物件上随势赋形，充满了非凡的想象力。可怜如今龙被庸俗了，将蛇称龙，将马称龙，将猪称龙，将鱼称龙，想象力枯竭，创造力丧失，民族精神的图腾一日复一日地削弱了它伟大的气质，这是龙之国度的人要浩叹的，连属龙相的我也恨恨不平了。

前几日，一位善戏谑的朋友见我，他先前叫我小贾，

a lizard, a chicken, a gecko or a salamander. Anything borrowed from a foreign culture ought to be delicate and enriching to the spirit. It is not the case that you should eat beef and grow as strong as cattle. Our ancestors concocted the image of the dragon, but it is a pity that their offspring have fallen into a regrettable habit. Whenever they invent something new, they take their lead from how the dragon was formed. They fuse together disparate sources. They make so many mistakes in so many fields. These days, we often hear people sigh and say: "They have surely inherited the seed of the dragon, so why do they give birth to a flea?"

The dragon has been around in China since antediluvian times. And yet our impression is that the dragon of the Qing Dynasty was embroidered upon the national flag, wheaeras in ordinary life it blotted out the sky and covered the earth. At the moment, when the Chinese discuss national tradition, the spiritual fountainhead cannot be traced back so very far. Nearsightedly, we only look back to the effete dynasties of the Ming and Qing. As a result, when we celebrate the Year of the Dragon, those who participate in the dragon and lion dance and those who beat drums and gongs wear neither the apparel of the Han and Tang Dynasties, nor even a Sun Yat-sen suit. They all dress in the vulgar colours and style of the Ming and Qing periods. Only one thing is missing. They do not have a greasy queue dangling behind their head. You may look around. How meagre and withered is the image of the dragon in modern times!

Originally, the dragon was fictitious, but those artists who painted dragons and artisans who crafted their likenesses served to make it more concrete as if real specimens existed under the heavens. They became like the cat on the *kang* and the dog guarding the back door. I appreciate the dragon carvings the ancients created. They are

数年后叫我老贾,现在开口叫我先生:"先生,该你腾云驾雾的时候了!"我说:"是吗,可你比我大,你该是先生的。"他说:"那怎么称谓你?"我说:"咱互称大人吧。大人虽是古称谓,但这称谓好,大人对着小人,从年龄上是对年长的尊重,从品德上是对君子的美誉。"他说:"这好啊,贾大人,瞧你这气色,明年龙当值,你若发达了,别忘了让我们也鸡犬升天哟!"我说:"但愿如此,但我要告诉你,世上还有一个鬼,它的名字叫日弄!"

说是说笑着,但我回来还是数次翻阅了字典中关于龙的条例解说,感觉属龙相的似乎也真有了龙性,臭皮囊也成了龙体,本来在医院挂了床号,每日去那里挂几瓶点滴的,就立即决定一九九九年十二月三十一日必须停止注射,让病留在前一个千年里去吧!在前一个千年的后近三十年里,我一直是文坛上的著名病人,躯体上、心灵上的病使我活得太难太累,如果近三十年里,尤其这十二年里一直在无奈而知趣地隐着、伏着,新一年里就该升腾显现,去呼风唤雨,去翻江倒海啊。今夜里满西安城里鼓乐喧天,人们如蜂如蚁涌向街头欢庆着新的千年,我和几位

a combination of the fish, the tiger, the horse, the snake, the deer and the pig. The dragons on the jade wares, bronze tripods, and weapons unearthed from the Western Zhou and Warring States times are all very simple and taut. They always display their shape and power in accordance with the artefact onto which they are incised. They exude extraordinary imagination as well. It is a pity that the dragon has been so vulgarised in the present. People call a snake or a pig a "dragon." Their imagination and creativity have abandoned them entirely. Day after day, the grandeur of the national totem has been eroded. The citizens of the dragon nation heave a deep sigh. Even I – a son of the Year of the Dragon – feel angry over this.

Several days ago, I ran into a friend who is apt to mock others. Before, he used to call me "Little Jia." Years later, he calls me "Old Jia."

Now that he has begun to address me as "sir," he said: "Sir, it's high time that you ride on the clouds and fog!"

I replied: "Is that so? But you are older than I am. I should call you 'sir'."

"Then how should I address you?"

I told him that we could call each other "your lordship". That may be an archaic form of address, but it is a good one. When a senior addresses a junior like this, it is meant to show deference to age. It also serves to praise the virtue of a gentleman.

He said: "That's nice, Jia, your lordship. How gallant you seem. Next year is the Year of the Dragon. If you prosper, don't forget to carry us dogs and chickens up to the heavens with you."

"I expect I shall, but I must tell you. A phantom is at large in the world. His name is Mr. Smart Arse!"

同样属龙相的朋友在家中小聚,我书写了"受命于天,寿而永昌"八个大字,这是公元前二百年时秦嬴政统一了中国所制的玺文,我说:"哇噻,时间过了二千年,原来这玺文是给我们刻铸的哟!"

Even though all of this was said lightheartedly, after coming home I consulted the dictionary several times to find the definition of "dragon". I came to feel that people born in the Year of the Dragon do indeed bear its character. My rancid body has transmogrified into that of a dragon. To begin with, I was admitted as an in-patient to be set up on a daily drip, but I immediately decided that from 31st December 1999 I would give this up and leave my illness behind with the passing millennium. For the last thirty years of this one thousand, I have been the famous sick man in the world of letters. My physical and spiritual malaise has rendered life too fatiguing and arduous. If in the past thirty years – especially the most recent twelve – I have been almlessly and sensibly living in hibernation like a hermit living sensibly and without the assitance of alms. When the New Year comes around, I should rise up and show myself, harnessing the winds and the rain and turn the rivers and the seas upside down. Tonight, loud music filled the air across Xi'an. Folks jammed into the streets like ants to enjoy the new millennium. A number of friends who are fellow dragons gathered together in my home. I wrote out eight large Chinese characters: "Fate offered by heaven, remains long and prosperous." These were the words cut into the Royal seal when Qin Shihuang unified the whole of China around two centuries before the birth of Christ.

I said: "Whoah, two millennia have past. The characters of the royal seal were actually carved by us!"

孤独地走向未来

好多人在说自己孤独,说自己孤独的人其实并不孤独。孤独不是受到了冷落和遗弃,而是无知己,不被理解。真正的孤独者不言孤独,偶尔做些长啸,如我们看到的兽。

弱者都是群居者,所以有芸芸众生。弱者奋斗的目的是转化为强者,像蛹向蛾的转化,但一旦转化成功了,就失去了原本满足和享受欲望的要求。国王是这样,名人是这样,巨富们的挣钱成了一种职业,种猪们的配种更不是为了爱情。

我见过相当多的郁郁寡欢者,也见过一些把皮肤和毛发弄得怪异的人,似乎要做孤独,这不是孤独,是孤僻,他们想成为六月的麦子,却在仅长出一尺余高就出穗孕粒,结的只是蝇子头般大的实。

Walking into the Future Alone

So many people claim that they are lonely. Actually those who say this out loud are not. Loneliness is not a matter of feeling the cold shoulder or being abandoned. Rather it comes about when you have no bosom friends and are misunderstood by others. Someone who is genuinely lonely will not mention this. Instead they will just heave long sighs like beasts.

The weak always congregate together. So many ordinary folks do just that. The weak struggle on in life with the purpose of becoming strong. Just as a pupa metamorphosing into a moth, once the change is complete, they promptly lose their original drive to satisfy and fulfil a desire. Monarchs, as well as celebrities, have been through this process too. For the super rich, making money is a profession, just like wild boars which spread their seed without needing love.

I have met plenty of melancholy and sullen people. I have also met some who have tattoos and dyed their hair in a very weird way. They try to put on an air of being lonely. This is not true loneliness but eccentricity. They want to be like wheat in June, shooting out ears when

每个行当里都有着孤独人,在文学界我遇到了一位。他的声名流布全国,对他的诽谤也铺天盖地,他总是默默,宠辱不惊,过着日子和进行着写作,但我知道他是孤独的。

"先生,"我有一天走近了他,说,"你想想,当一碗肉大家都在眼睛盯着并努力去要吃到,你却首先将肉端跑了,能避免不被群起而攻之吗?"

他听了我的话,没有说是或者不是,也没有停下来握一下我的手,突然间泪流满脸。

"先生,先生……"我撵着他还要说。

"我并不孤独。"他说,匆匆地走掉了。

我以为我要成为他的知己,但我失败了,那他为什么要流泪呢?"我并不孤独"又是什么意思呢?

一年后这位作家又出版了新作,在书中的某一页上我读

they are only one foot high. Their grain is no bigger than the head of a fly.

There are lonely people in every walk of life. I met one such person in the literary field. He was famous all over China, and the slander spouted about him could blot out the sky and cover up the earth. However, he remained silent. Regardless of whether he was being flattered or trampled upon, he carried on his daily life and writing. I knew that he was lonely.

One day I approached him and said: "Sir, just you think about it. When everyone else's eyes are coveting a bowl of meat, you grab it and run away. How can you avoid being attacked by all sides?"

After hearing my words, he neither said yes nor no, nor did he stop and shake hands with me. All of a sudden his face was drenched with tears.

"Sir, sir!" I chased after him.

"I am not lonely." With those words he left in a hurry.

I thought I could become his bosom friend, though failed. Why did he shed tears? What did he mean by "I am not lonely"?

A year later, this writer published another book. On one of its pages I found eight words "Great saints behave prosaically, great people act cautiously." I finally understood: the world is never quick to make somebody feel lonely. Communal living requires a kind of balance. Jealousy triggers off slander, homocide, humiliation, attacks and persecution. If you do not stand out of the crowd, you will remain

到了"圣贤庸行，大人小心"八个字，我终于明白了，尘世并不会轻易让一个人孤独的，群居需要一种平衡，嫉妒而引发的诽谤、扼杀、打击和迫害，你若不再脱颖，你将平凡；你若继续走，走，终于使众生无法赶超了，众生就会向你欢呼和崇拜，尊你是神圣。神圣是真正的孤独。

走向孤独的人难以接受怜悯和同情。

common. If you toil on and on, the others can no longer catch up with or surpass you. They are then compelled to worship and applaud you, exalting you as some divine being. Those who are divine are truly lonely.

It is extremely hard for a man walking towards loneliness to accept the pity and sympathy of others.